THE THIRD SYZYGY

THE THIRD SYZYGY

By

Stanford Apseloff

Illustrations by Michael Cheval

OHIO DISTINCTIVE PUBLISHING

Columbus, Ohio

Published by Ohio Distinctive Publishing.

ISBN 978-1-936772-22-3
Library of Congress Control Number: 2019910393

For my children, and yours.

Author's Note

The magic of books is created in part by our imagination, the unique way each of us interprets written words to create images of characters, places, and events. A book with illustrations adds a foundation for our perceptions and interpretations, and brings greater depth to our experience with the storyline.

Illustrations for books are usually created by artists who take direction from the author or editors; the artists themselves remain outside the story. This book is different. Here the artist is Michael Cheval, the internationally acclaimed painter of dreams. In this story, the paintings of Michael Cheval alter reality, foreshadow the future, and provide a gateway between the waking world and that of dreams. You will travel across two worlds where only imagination and the art of Michael Cheval can take you. I hope you enjoy the journey as much as we did.

Contents

Any two-year-old will tell you that dreams are real as rainbows. Grown-ups, when they're awake, don't know this simple truth.

The Museum

The museum guard eyed Laney disapprovingly, his lips parting in preparation for a sharp rebuke. Laney's bubblegum popped as she leaned closer to the artwork, chewing with her mouth open.

"Grandpa paintings," she announced, turning away from a Vermeer masterpiece. She popped another bubble, and headed into the next gallery, clicking her boot heels on the marble floor. "More grandpa paintings," she mumbled. Her feet carried her into a hallway as she searched for the front of the building.

Laney's mother and kid brother stood patiently in the middle of the atrium, not surprised that Laney's shortcut through the seventeenth-century wing added an extra ten minutes to their rendezvous.

"There you are!" her mom scolded. "Are you taking notes? You know how important this paper is."

Laney sighed.

"Open mind, Laney, and a little bit of effort—it's not that hard. You could write something about that Picasso quote: '*Everything you can imagine is real.*'"

"How about, 'Everything I learn is lame.'" Laney's interest in art had been squashed at an early age when she drew on the dining room walls—what else does a four-year-old do with crayons? The colorful tools of childhood had been unceremoniously snatched from her little hands, and after a swat on the behind, she was sent to her room. "History, geography, art—who cares? I'll never use any of it."

"Maybe you'd be happier living with cavemen. All you'd need to learn is how to build a fire."

"Yeah, and then I could draw on the walls and not get punished." Laney looked for a reaction, but her mother seemed not to remember "the crayon incident."

Laney popped her gum. "Ryan, what do you think? Pretty boring, huh?"

"I like the history museum."

Laney nodded. "Dead animals, shrunken heads, poison arrows—what's not to like?"

Laney's mom rolled her eyes. "There weren't any shrunken heads."

"There could be," Laney argued. "Those spears and arrows were real. Get stuck and you hallucinate, and then you die. Lovely stuff for little kids."

Ryan tapped his foot in a small puddle of melted snow from his boots. "Mommy says we can get gummy bears when we're done."

"You and your gummy bears," said Laney. "Nasty stuff."

"Shhhh—quiet. It's Vivaldi." The violin solo from *The Four Seasons – 'Winter'* streamed through the hall, leaving faint echoes in its wake.

"Elevator music," Laney declared.

"It's like Mrs. Whitfield's music," Ryan chimed in.

Mrs. Whitfield—the kindergarten teacher who talked to everyone like they were five years old, wore pointy wicked-witch shoes, and at recess clutched a giant, red golf umbrella as if it were her broom.

"You know that woman's crazy—everyone says so." Laney wasn't being mean, just making an observation. Mrs. Whitfield, for her part, knew that children past the age of six recognized her peculiarities, and she tended to avoid them whenever possible. Older kids made fun of her behind her back, often within earshot but always out of reach.

"I like Mrs. Whitfield."

Of course—Ryan liked everyone, even the kids who teased him because his feet didn't point the way they should.

"Can we go now?" Ryan whined.

Laney's mother glanced at her watch. "It's time for kindergarten. Laney, when I get back, we'll practice your driving, if the snow doesn't get any worse."

"I don't mind the snow."

"I do. We don't want any accidents before you get your license. I'll be back in an hour, and then we'll see." She yawned. Ryan's nightmare had awakened the whole house the night before. Even Laney had gotten out of bed to see what all the commotion was about. "It's just a dream," Ryan's mother had assured him, hugging his trembling body. "Dreams aren't real."

But Ryan had insisted: "It's real—the monster's coming! Laney, you were there—tell Mommy you're going to fight the monster."

Laney, standing in the doorway still half asleep, had made no reply.

Ryan and Laney had gone back to sleep after that, but not their mother. Now she yawned again, before offering Laney parting words of wisdom: "Take notes, and don't touch anything!"

"Bye," said Laney, having no intention of taking notes. "Don't be late—it's a paper, not a thesis."

Ryan tugged his mother's arm, and Laney thought, *It's like Major pulling on his leash.*

Laney wandered out of the atrium, through a narrow corridor, and into one of the neoclassical galleries. *Not interesting,* she thought, and walked out to the now-empty hallway. She stood alone with the echo of fading footsteps, the lunch-hour retreat. At midday the museum cafeteria attracted patrons like ants on a mission. Tables filled and lines formed for croissant sandwiches and real lemonade, and on Saturdays the best key lime pie anywhere. But today was not Saturday, and Laney needed to find artwork for a term paper, something with an obvious "eight printed pages" story.

"You'll find a painting that talks to you," Mrs. Rollins had said. "You need to see it for real, not in a book. Reproductions lose the magic of the art. You must experience a painting as it existed the moment it was created—then you will know."

Know what? Laney had thought. Mrs. Rollins had gone on and on about a painting she had seen of someone screaming—something about pain flowing from each stroke of the brush. Mrs. Rollins had issues, Laney thought. But Mrs. Rollins liked Laney, and if she could come up with a topic to write about, she was pretty sure she'd get a good grade.

So she headed down the hall toward the next century—Monet and Renoir. But the impressionist paintings didn't impress—*like elevator music on canvas*, she thought. So down the next hallway she went, up to an overhead banner that read, "Michael Cheval's Dreams—A Surreal Treat, October 23 - January 31." But today was October 22, and the door past the banner had a sign that read: "Closed. Employees Only."

As she approached the sign, the door opened and two employees came out—it was the lunch hour, after all. The woman chatted at a highly caffeinated rate about the distinction between surrealism and absurdity, while the man nodded and smiled and stole quick glances at the woman's attributes. Neither of the two noticed that the door behind failed to click shut. Laney waited until the museum officials rounded the corner, and then entered the room.

The Michael Cheval exhibit appeared ready to roll, each painting expertly hung and leveled. Spotlights shined in the otherwise dim room.

Laney's gaze swept across the Cheval paintings. Children chased echoes.

Music turned into butterflies. A woman and her violin dripped like honey, and a blind man painted a picture.

More than a dozen paintings lined the walls. Laney stepped up to the nearest one—two heavenly bodies dancing a tango. "The moon and the sun," she mused. Beside that, a swan-faced man romance a blue-haired lady who stared through their varnished surface with a look of, "What are you doing out there?"

"Not eight pages," Laney mumbled.

She turned her gaze toward *Magic of Trivial Illusions*, where a magician transformed a deck of cards into doves in flight. Beneath the painting, something on the floor caught her eye—she picked it up and turned it over—a joker. She put it in her coat pocket.

She walked past *Blind Inspiration* and *Honey-Sweet Serenade* and came to . . . *The Muse*—a woman leaning gently on a musician's shoulder, pouring liquid into his head via a series of water pipes. Laney followed the flow with her eyes, and then heard a drip-drip-drip—water droplets splashing a marble floor. She looked down, and a second later another drop announced its arrival. She looked up, but the towering ceiling gave away no clues. "Weird," she said, stepping away from the puddle.

A few more steps—past an emergency exit—*Love Hunter II.* Forest shadows reached across the snow-covered field to the huntress, standing ready, her weapon of choice a lute transforming at its neck into a crossbow—cocked. The steely woman peered over her shoulder toward Laney as if responding to a sound or smell that only a skilled woman of the woods might detect. Laney locked eyes with the huntress, and for a split second she was there, standing in the snow, holding her breath. She blinked, and the magic disappeared. The woman's keen eyes softened, gazing vacantly from a face surrounded by thick paprika curls aglow in the sinking sun. Rabbits hopped from folds in the huntress's satin skirt—they sat and looked about like warm, bundled children introduced to snow for the first time.

Laney moved closer, and her foot kicked something camouflaged by the dimly lit floor: an arrow, like the one in the painting. She picked it up. "Hmmm . . . props?" She looked back at the previous painting, and the water dripping from the ceiling—and then she felt the prick on her finger, the point of the arrow effortlessly penetrating as she carelessly touched the tip. Her hands jerked, and the arrow clattered onto the floor. A drop of blood formed on her fingertip, and she sucked it. "Agggh!" It hurt more than she expected, like a hornet sting when she and the neighborhood kids used to throw rocks at the huge paper nests. She shook her hand to fling away the pain.

She stepped away, and when she looked up, a man in uniform stood before her, staring through a frame as if looking in from a window. He flashed a hint of

A few more steps—past an emergency exit—Love Hunter II.

a smile, as if he knew something she didn't. He wore a hat with a pendulum clock and the letter "Z"—what did it mean? She felt her eyes drawn toward the pendulum clock, and as she stared, she fancied she heard it ticking. Clearly it was ticking. She stepped back, wondering, *How can that be?* And then she saw—the ticking came from above, a clock on the wall.

She stepped away, but the man in uniform gazed after her, all the way to . . . *Midsummer Chirr.* A field nymph in a headdress of meadow reeds and wildflowers played a miniature violin to the delight of two crickets. The image looked so real Laney fancied she could reach out and touch it—for real. The details were so fine they fooled the human eye. Even as she tilted her head, the surface appeared three dimensional—the nearest cricket seeming to change perspective. And then it moved!

Laney jerked back with a gasp. The cricket stepped forward and lifted a wing. Laney's eyes darted across the painting, trying to understand. A cricket, yes, but otherwise brushstrokes, nothing but brushstrokes, a painting flat in a frame—with one very real cricket escaping the fate of fall's first freeze.

Laney lowered her chin and sighed—she felt lightheaded. Maybe skipping lunch wasn't such a good idea. She backed away from the painting, looking down at her feet as if to make sure they were on solid ground. She passed by a couple more paintings and headed across the room, toward the exit. She was almost there when she did a double take—*Stairway to Heaven* had caught her eye. A freestanding staircase ascended through an alien-looking sky, toward the light. At the foot of the staircase, a tailor affixed angel-sized monarch wings onto a girl who looked . . . exactly like Laney!

The room began to spin. Laney looked left and right, trying to lock her gaze on anything that might make everything stand still. A bench—she stumbled toward it. Nausea washed over her. She spat her gum onto the floor. The moment stretched, like a dream that wouldn't end. The clock on the wall echoed through the vacant hall—louder, slower, and for an instant time seemed to stop.

"Breathe!" Laney commanded herself as she clutched the bench. She bent forward and blood rushed to her brain. Her head began to clear, the spinning room winding down like a merry-go-round as the music stops and the horses take one last leap up and down. Finally the gallery stood still, paintings firmly affixed to immovable walls. *It's the wrong museum for poison arrows*, she thought. *It's just a prop, all of it just props.*

Before she could think another thought, an alarm pierced the silence.

"Get out! Get out! Everybody out!" someone yelled from the hallway beyond the door. The sound of hurried steps and panicked shouts came from both sides of the gallery. Laney shook her head, stood up, and ran to the emergency exit beside *Love Hunter II.* With a quick glance at the huntress, she pushed open the door and stepped out into the cold. The door clanged shut behind her.

Swirling snow engulfed Laney, stinging her face. She squinted and shielded her eyes, looking to find whoever might be nearby, someone who might tell her what was happening. Snowflakes dived toward her, and she could see nothing else. "Hey . . . wow! Anyone here? Hello!" No answer. She yelled louder as she leaned forward into the blinding snow, reaching with one hand. *It's only October,* she thought, *how can there be this much snow?* She circled one way and then the other, all the while calling out, but no one answered. Soon she had lost all sense of direction. *Where's the building?* she wondered. She looked down at her bootprints in the ankle-deep snow—markers in a maze, but slowly disappearing in the swirling wind. She would have to hurry. She followed them back, carefully where they crisscrossed—until suddenly they stopped. She reached forward—nothing but air. She stepped past the first footprints with her hands in front of her, expecting, hoping, to feel a door. She yelled, "HELP! HELP!" but her voice was no match for the strength of the wind, and she heard not even an echo in reply. She yelled again, even louder, and strained to see anything through the relentless snowflakes. There was nothing to see.

Into the Forest

Laney's voice finally gave out, and she swallowed to soothe her throat. She looked down at the trampled snow, the footprints filling with fresh flakes, and she was reminded of another snowfall long ago: Laney was five, and the winter festival was in full swing—her parents had taken her to witness the sights and sounds of the season. Had she wandered off, or had her parents somehow left without her?—suddenly she was alone, as any child is in a crowd of strangers. She remembered the snowflakes, so thick that they fell in clumps. She swallowed her fear and wandered down the main aisle to the Christmas tree farm, where happy families inspected evergreens of all shapes and sizes. The smell of fresh-cut pine filled the air. Wherever she roamed, she imagined each step leading closer to her parents—where were they hiding?—or were they looking for her? In and out of the trees she wandered, up and down the rows. And then suddenly a familiar face, Mrs. McKensie from next door asking, "Where are your parents?"

Where was everybody? This made no sense. The museum at noon held hundreds of people, and sidewalks and parking lots surrounded the building—not endless fields of snow. All signs of civilization had suddenly disappeared. But then Laney remembered her cell phone. She fumbled with cold hands in her shoulder bag until her fingers found it.

The phone searched for reception—and continued to search. "Come on!" Laney pleaded, but it would not connect. She looked at the time—exactly twelve noon. *That can't be right,* she thought. *It should be way past noon. Where am I?* Mom would be looking for her soon, calling her cell phone—what then? Laney put her phone in her coat pocket. Her hands hurt, and she clasped them together, like two halves of a broken cup. They were dangerously cold. Laney reached into her bag again and retrieved a pair of gloves.

The wind began to subside. Snow fell like feathers, huge flakes piling quickly. But without the swirling wind, Laney could see into the distance. Snow extended to the horizon in all directions—except one. To the east a tree line appeared, like a ship in the fog. She wondered how far—maybe a mile, maybe two. *Should be warmer there, out of the wind,* she thought. *Can't stay here.* She flipped her coat collar up and headed toward the trees.

After some time, Laney looked back, seeing her footprints vanish into the distance. She tried her cell phone again—nothing, and it still said twelve o'clock. *This can't be happening!* she kept thinking, but nonetheless it was. The wind picked up again, and the cold began to numb her thoughts and fears. Soon she lost track of time and distance, and simply put one foot in front of the other.

The forest drew nearer. The treetops rose, and the woods revealed a majesty that had been hidden by the falling snow. Evergreens and birches reached toward the sky in a century-long race toward sunlight, while brush sprawled about the base of the trees and spewed from the forest.

At the edge of the forest, the shadow of the great trees fell upon Laney, and a chill ran through her. *People get lost in the woods,* she thought.

But I'm already lost.

She looked around at the endless snow, a nothingness devoid of possibilities and hope. She would choose the mystery and danger of the woods.

Laney stepped into the brush, trampling what she could not push aside. The thicket of bramble clawed and clutched her coat, but she pushed forward, snapping sticks and dead branches, kicking up leaves and snow. With a final yank and twist, she tore free and stepped beneath the canopy of trees.

The ground sloped downward, welcoming Laney. Struggling shrubs that crept along the forest floor lay bare, offering little resistance as she moved among the trees. A carpet of leaves and patchy snow hid rocks and ruts, but vines stretching from the forest floor to distant boughs invited her to steady herself.

She tried to stay near the boundary of the forest, but in spite of her efforts to keep the clearing in sight, the terrain guided her away. The ground rose sharply near the forest boundary, and she found herself giving way to the contours of the land.

Roots turned her feet. Branches clawed her face. *Forests have trails,* she thought. *Keep walking—find a trail.*

Aimlessly she wandered, ever deeper into the forest, the endless procession of trees as timeless as an ocean. Hours slipped by. But then up ahead . . . daylight.

She pushed through branches of lesser trees and stepped into sunshine so bright it made her squint. But there before her stood neither civilization nor an end to the forest. A vast ravine lay almost at her feet, and she stepped away from the dizzying depth. She caught her breath and followed the ravine with her eyes, watching it wind through the forest out of sight in both directions. But she could see that the cliff descended to her right—she would go that way, with the wind at her back.

The ravine twisted and turned, and after a time she began to wonder whether she had indeed chosen the downward path. She kept a comfortable distance from the edge of the cliff, weaving in and out of the trees that dared grow close to the edge. The breeze along the relatively open expanse helped push her forward, but the biting cold seemed to blow right through her—and then a tremendous gust almost knocked her off her feet. She staggered forward, digging her heels into the snow, but the whistling wind faded like the end of a long last breath. And there Laney stood in a sudden calm amidst a complete absence of living sounds, other than her own. No birds overhead, no squirrel rustling dead leaves—just silence beneath her rhythmic breathing. She took a step, hearing and feeling the snow pack under her boot, and in that moment she wondered if anyone would ever see her footprints, if she would ever be found.

Laney shuddered from head to toe—but she felt something more, a tremor beneath her feet—growing, coming toward her. Her imagination might have conjured a stampede of elephants, but instinctively she knew—this was an earthquake!

Her eyes darted this way and that—then up. The canopy lay thick with ice and snow.

Trees swayed. Branches snapped. Slabs of snow-ice pounded the earth. Laney jumped back—toward the ravine.

The edge—nowhere to go. Earth and snow tumbled into the abyss. A sapling—she grabbed hold. Branches fell like missiles. A tree uprooted—coming at Laney. The sight and sound filled her mind.

She let go of the sapling, and all she could think was . . . *This is it!*

Down she fell, into the ravine. The rush of air carried away both hope and fear. A calm enveloped her—the cold disappeared, the sound of crashing trees vanished, and time melted like a Salvador Dali clock.

Desperation

In an explosion of snow, Laney slammed onto a ledge, breaking her fall. She opened her mouth, gasping, fighting for air. Her chest heaved again and again but her lungs wouldn't fill, until finally they relented, and cold air rushed into her body. She lay on her back staring upward through a tangle of branches—the fallen tree that had threatened to crush her now dangled its crown in her face. She reached to push the tips away. Her head throbbed, but the snow had largely broken her fall. Tomorrow she could count the bruises, but now she needed to find a way off the ledge. She sat up among the branches, and turned to look to the bottom of the ravine. Hundreds of feet below, boulders and broken limbs lay scattered—up was the only way out.

Laney patted her coat to check for her phone. Gone! She shoved her hands into both pockets—not there. She searched the ledge, crawling, sweeping the snow and debris with her arms. Then she peered over the edge—*It's down there!*

A wave of despair washed over her, and for a moment she couldn't move. But then a single thought screamed—*GET UP!*

She moved away from the edge, then tightened her shoulder bag across her body and reached high into the tangle of branches. They bent and flexed, but she held tight. Pulling and kicking, she made her way up.

The top of the cliff came within reach, and she pulled herself onto firm ground. She retreated to the trees and then lay on her back to catch her breath.

As she gazed at the canopy and the patchy light of the sky, she felt as though she had been in the forest for ages. Thoughts of before receded like a vanishing dream. Only *now* mattered.

She got to her feet and started walking. Forward, wherever that might be—forward must be the way. She plunged into the deepening shadows.

A chill beyond cold settled onto the forest, and Laney huffed a mist like dragon's breath. Her arm swung as rigid as a clock pendulum, forcing her freezing feet to keep pace. All the while slivers of sunlight danced among the trees, flitting through gaps in outstretched limbs, disappearing behind trunks and then springing out again one step later. Shadows bent by the breeze played tricks on the eyes, creating an illusion of movements among the trees, as if silent animals scampered in the shadows.

On and on Laney trekked, becoming mesmerized by the endless passing of trees and the methodical beat of her boots. And then she heard something that stopped her dead in her tracks—music! Faint, carried by the wind, it faded in and out of the breeze. She held her breath. Violins, orchestra music, and had she not seemed eons removed from the earlier part of her day, she might have recognized it as the same music that had delighted her mother at the museum. *Where can it be?* she thought, straining to peg a direction. *Straight ahead*, she decided as she turned her head from side to side. She ran headlong toward the sound, but as fast as she ran, the music seemed to retreat, like a desert mirage. She stopped and held her breath to listen, to make sure the music hadn't changed direction. "WHERE ARE YOU?" she yelled, and getting no response, she again raced toward the faint melody of the violin. Finally out of breath, she stopped to

listen for the music over the sound of her rasping lungs. Still straight ahead, but even farther in the distance.

Half walking, half trotting, she willed her legs to obey. She slipped and stumbled as her foot landed on a patch of ice, and as she looked down and then back up again, she realized that she now stood upon a path.

She looked down the path in both directions—no tire tracks, no footprints, no telltale signs of civilization, but it lay flat and clear in sharp contrast to the rest of the forest floor. The music disappeared for a moment, but then it seemed to resume down the path. She forced herself to run.

The path dipped and curved, but always it seemed in the direction of the music. But then after a brief crescendo, the music faded . . . and disappeared. She searched and listened in all directions, straining to hear something beyond the faint rustle of the breeze. "I'M HERE!" she yelled, as loud as her lungs would allow. She heard nothing in return.

She continued down the path, racing against the setting sun. The waning light darted in and out among the trees, playing tricks on her eyes. But then real movements began to accompany the illusions of the light.

Laney saw the first rabbit out of the corner of her eye, but more quickly followed, darting between the trees. At least a dozen scampered on both sides of the trail. They began to race ahead of Laney, as if they were guiding her forward. Soon they disappeared into the distance.

As the sun set, darkness seeped into the woods. Although her eyes adjusted to the failing light, Laney knew soon she would be unable to see. Her heart beat fast but faint, as if it might flutter and cease. Straggling thoughts of home, family, and friends disappeared as completely as if they had never existed. The past and the future, what was and might be, ceased as if the dimension of time had collapsed to a single point. The present. The mist of each halting breath. The whistle and rustle of the wind. The creeping darkness. And then, in spite of her indomitable spirit, each step came slower than the last, until she simply looked into the distance wondering whether she had in fact finally given up.

But then amidst the deepening darkness she spied a faint glimmer, through the trees, just a little off the path. Her eyes perhaps played tricks on her—but each time she blinked, the light reappeared. She stumbled toward it, weaving her way through the trees. Another light appeared beside the first, and then another—windows in a cottage! And suddenly the pristine air no longer carried just the scent of fresh pine—a breeze delivered a faint whiff of chimney smoke.

The cottage sat at the bottom of a steep hill, such that the snow from the slope mounded and flowed onto the roof, creating the appearance that the cottage belonged to the hillside. The natural wood facing flecked with snow and ice blended into the trees, but light shone from the windows like a jack-o'-lantern leering through the forest.

Hope brought tears to Laney's eyes. She reached the cottage and pounded numb fists like hammers upon the oak door, crying "Help me! Please help me!" She grabbed the door knocker and slammed it onto its brass plate again and again.

The sharp blasts of the knocker resonated through the oak door, and a rumbling followed from above. She looked up into the darkness, not realizing that ice and snow piled high on the roof had lost its grip. As she stood at the threshold of safety, the wintery mass crashed upon her, and Laney's reality vanished as if it were a dream.

Shaka

Laney awoke to the sound of heavy breathing, so close she could feel the warm, moist exhalations on her face. She opened her eyes, and a large sled dog stood over her, mouth open, eyes fixed upon hers.

"Tak will not bite—not unless I tell him to," came a voice from across the room, a woman seated at a table cracking pairs of walnuts in her hand as easily as if they were robin's eggs. She dropped them into a pile she had been working on

Her leprechaun-green eyes scanned every inch of Laney.

and came toward Laney. "What do you think, Tak?" she said to the dog. "Not what we expected."

The dog stepped back beside his master. The woman came closer, and Laney couldn't help but notice her natural beauty. Chafing from cold and wind accented the woman's high cheekbones, and a scattering of faint freckles matched a curly head of hair as full as a lion's mane. Her leprechaun-green eyes scanned every inch of Laney.

"Where am I?" Laney pushed herself up to a seated position at the far side of the bench where she lay, and looked about the room. A fireplace crackled and hissed as flames danced upon the wood, and several portable lanterns cast light and shadows across the room. Another dog the size of a small bear sat in the far corner.

"You are at my home," replied the woman, "but how you came to be here—that is a mystery! You must have journeyed through the West Woods, but no one does that—not anymore. Few go beyond the new growth of Tarzetta Trail, and fewer still dare tread upon the paths of old. Who are you?"

Who are you?—the rote answer to that question suddenly required a moment of thought. And in that instant of searching for the handle of that most ingrained memory, Laney realized that the handle, all handles, had been replaced by a vast emptiness, as if she were looking across the surface of an endless sea, trying to discern what lay beneath. She felt no panic, just confusion, as if waking from a dream and not knowing where she lay, not really knowing anything, and waiting that brief moment for awareness and memory to return. But the moment persisted.

"Where am I?" Laney repeated, as if that answer would open the gate to all others.

"You are at the last dwelling on Tarzetta Trail," the woman replied, her hand on her hip and her chin in the air. "I am Shaka, the Guardian of Tarzetta Trail, the heir of the arrows, the dreamer of dreams. Who are you, and why have you come?" She tossed her head, and the rust-colored curls bounced like springs.

Laney looked about the room again and then shook her head. "I don't remember . . . anything.

"How did I get here?" she mumbled to herself, but she had no answer. Everything about herself had become a mystery. She remembered only knowledge that present circumstances might pull from the depths of her mind. Her life's adventures, her likes and dislikes, her hopes and dreams, and all her memories outside this room remained out of reach.

"Your coming has been foretold," said Shaka, "yet I am surprised. No staff, no crystals, and I had to rescue *you* at my front door. Sorceress from the West, you are not what I expected."

Sorceress from the West? What's this woman saying? Laney's personal memory hid somewhere out of reach, but still she possessed rational thought, and some practical knowledge. She knew how to communicate with this woman, and she wasn't frightened by the dog. "Sorceress from the West"—that didn't ring true.

Breathe, Laney thought. *Whatever's happening, just go with it—you're safe, you're warm.* She took a few deep breaths—and then wrinkled her nose. "What's that smell?" she said.

"Dogs. Dogs smell, but they care not, and neither should you."

"No, not that—food?" The smell touched upon something in Laney's memory, but she couldn't place it.

"Soup—you are welcome to what remains—not much. I expected no visitors."

Laney's stomach ached for food, but the smell made her eyes water—what would it do if she ate it? Again she wrinkled her nose.

"As you wish," said Shaka. She turned to the table near the center of the room. "You carried a sack with strange provisions for a journey such as yours." The bag lay overturned on the table, its contents spread about. Shaka reached for one of the items and held it up for Laney.

"You put that on your lips," said Laney, pleased that she vaguely recognized the small container.

Shaka gave Laney a questioning look.

"It's not important," said Laney. She now noticed that Shaka wore no makeup of any kind—freckles blended into her complexion like distant stars fading into oblivion. Laney tried to read Shaka's expressions, but the keen eyes and occasional raised eyebrow gave away nothing. Who was this woman? She looked strong—chiseled jaw and a neck graceful and muscular like a python. And she had big dogs.

Shaka put down the lip gloss and picked up a brown paper bag, opened it, and pulled out a partially thawed ham-and-cheese sandwich sealed in a plastic sandwich bag. She turned it over, examining both sides, seemingly puzzled by either the sandwich or its packaging. Laney motioned for Shaka to bring it to her. Shaka obliged and then watched with curiosity as Laney devoured the food and cast aside the plastic bag.

"Your adventures coming here must make for a fine tale." Shaka raised an eyebrow hoping for a response, but Laney just shook her head.

"No staff, no crystals, but you did bring this . . ." Shaka continued, pushing aside a book, reluctant to touch it. The title read *Chemistry*.

"What is it?" Laney asked and stopped chewing.

"I do not know—'tis not mine to open."

Laney got to her feet to come take a look. Her head pounded with each heartbeat, and she felt weak and faint, but she had to see this clue.

She opened the book to the middle, and then flipped back through several pages before reading aloud a passage: "The mole fraction of a solute is equal to the number of moles of the solute divided by the total number of moles of all the components in the solution."

Laney closed the book. "Moles?" she said looking up at Shaka.

"Moles, toads, newts—a book of spells no doubt," Shaka replied.

Laney opened the book to the inside front cover. A name had been hastily scrawled: Larey—no, Laney. She traced the name with her finger and said it out loud, trying to make it feel familiar. But nothing about it clicked in her brain.

"And there is this that I found in your outer garment," said Shaka as she pushed aside the bag to reveal a playing card joker. "This imp—who might he be, smiling like this?"

But Laney did not know and could only shake her head. She reached for the shoulder bag and upended it, hoping for more clues about herself, but nothing remained inside, except two gummy bears that Ryan had generously deposited sometime in the past. Now upside down in the bag, the bears released their sticky grip and tumbled onto the table. Shaka leaned forward to see what she had missed in her earlier inspection of the bag. "Little bears?" she said, and she studied Laney for a reaction. "What is the purpose of little bears?"

But Laney, equally puzzled, did not respond. Instead she pushed aside an empty notebook revealing a child's crayon drawing beneath, a crude semblance of a smiling girl surrounded by red hearts, with the printed words, "Laney" and "Love Ryan" scrawled in bold, red print.

As she held the crayon drawing, she glanced back at the book. "I'm . . . Laney," she said, as much a question as a statement.

Shaka studied Laney's reaction. "Is Ryan your son? Or maybe your grandson? You look unspoiled by the toll of many winters, but a sorceress might have such powers. You could be as old as the tallest trees in the West Woods."

Laney willed the drawing to spark a recollection, but it was no use. She shook her head.

"Strange powers brought you here," said Shaka, "either yours or the hand of fate. Nobody comes through a snowstorm from the West Woods—except in the tales of old. Your coming has been foretold, in stories and in my dreams. A blind sorceress to stand against the black fog of the West Woods, to purge it forever and break the spell that turned the wolves against us. Stories and dreams—only the wise can truly understand all that they foretell, but there is no denying that you are here. Blind in a different way no doubt, but you came from the West Woods with your sorceress' book—only a fool would ignore the prophesies."

"I don't know why I'm here, but I'm not a sorceress. I'm just . . . me."

Shaka smiled a soothing smile. "You truly are lost—blind to who you are. You came here alone, and neither of us knows how—but that we shall discover in the days ahead. Now you must rest. Tomorrow we shall start our journey."

Laney wanted to protest, but overcome with exhaustion, she couldn't find the right words. She looked about the room—wood furniture, logs for the well-tended fireplace—nothing she didn't understand. The simplicity comforted her.

"Tomorrow we go west," said Shaka. "Our destiny. But tonight you must rest and regain your strength. Tak and Gallia shall watch over you. You have nothing to fear in my home."

I need a plan, thought Laney. *One way or another, I'm going home in the morning.*

Arrows and Crystals

Tak nudged Laney until she stirred. If she had dreamed, the visions escaped before her first wakeful breath. She sat up, remembering the conversation from the night before, but nothing prior. She felt a cold breeze and turned to see Shaka standing in the open doorway to the outside. Shaka seemed to be sniffing the air.

"The storm has passed. The wind's breath blows clear—time to load the packs." Shaka came inside and closed the door.

"We need to find someone who knows me." said Laney as she stood up to face Shaka.

"There is no one here who will know you," Shaka replied. "Farrouton is two days' journey to the east. We must go west."

"West—are there people there?"

"I do not know," said Shaka.

"I'm not going to the middle of nowhere," Laney insisted.

Shaka approached, put a hand on Laney's shoulder, and looked kindly into her eyes. "You are not from Farrouton, nor Parmelth, nor any village as far as I have ever traveled. What you wear is strange to me. These teeth that you pull open and shut . . ." Shaka pointed to the zipper on Laney's coat, ". . . and these pouches that close with a touch and cry out when they are opened . . ." Shaka motioned toward the coat pockets with Velcro fasteners. "No, your home is as much a mystery to me as it is to you. But you are not here by chance. You have powers that you know not, but you shall find them."

Laney shook her head. "No, you're wrong."

"When the time comes, you will know," Shaka insisted. "Until then, we shall travel together, and I shall protect you."

"Do I have a choice?" asked Laney.

"You may go where you wish," said Shaka with a wave of her hand. "But how shall you find your way? If you start your journey with me, you may find that your feet take you where they are meant to go."

"And if I am meant to go elsewhere?"

"Even a bottle adrift in the sea will find its way to land," said Shaka. "I shall help you only so long as our travels are meant to be together. You have my word."

Laney could see confidence in Shaka's eyes and hear a ring of truth in her voice.

"Nothing shall greet you to the east," Shaka continued, "but to the west, destiny awaits! Before our journey ends, you shall have all your answers, and I shall have mine. My mother and her mother's mother foretold of a clearing in the heart of the West Woods, a place where dreams are real and prophesies may be fulfilled. We shall go there, and you shall see."

Laney held Shaka's gaze but made no response.

"If you knew more about the West Woods, you would realize how magical it is that you are here," said Shaka. "The syzygy will happen in ten days. It is a rare opportunity. The timing is not by chance."

"Siza-what?" asked Laney.

Shaka threw up her hands. "Syzygy—the heavenly alignment, the dance between the sun and the moon—the magical time when anything is possible!" she exclaimed. "This syzygy is special. Often the moon struts its brightest glory or chases the sun, but this syzygy is different. This is a magical syzygy where the moon shall catch the sun and hold her, and when that happens anything is possible! This is the third such syzygy since I became Guardian of Tarzetta Trail. The first two did not align with the teachings of the prophecy, but this third one is different—different because of my dreams, and different because you are here.

There is magic in the air, and it will grow as the day of the syzygy draws near. Do you not feel it? This third syzygy is the one! There has been none like it in my lifetime, and I expect there shall be no other before my days are gone. Victory against the black fog and the curse that it brings must happen during this syzygy, or not at all—now is our chance. We shall go to the clearing."

Laney shook her head. "That's not what I need."

Shaka sighed. "You know me not, but you must trust what I say. Look into my eyes, and tell me whether I speak the truth."

Laney could feel the intensity of Shaka's stare. "I know you say what you believe—I just don't know what I believe. Where is this clearing?"

"Several days' journey, at the least. I shall lead us as quickly as you can travel. The syzygy arrives in ten days—we must not be late." Shaka squeezed Laney's shoulder and nodded as if the matter had been decided. "I must ready the packs," she said. "We shall travel light, and I shall carry the heavier load. Yesterday you came from the west, and today we go back. Toward your home?—I do not know, but you have walked these woods before."

Retracing steps—that appealed to Laney—but the wilderness, not so much. "I don't know anything about the woods," she said.

"I do," Shaka replied as she began stuffing garments and provisions into two packs. "I know more about the West Woods than any but the wise."

"The wise?" asked Laney.

"Yes, they know more than you can imagine, and more than we can understand."

"Where are they?" Laney perked up, grasping at this possibility.

"The wise travel far and wide, for how else could they obtain the wisdom of the land?"

"But how do you find them?" Laney persisted.

"One will find us, if need be, on the road. We shall see. I have heard that parts of the West Woods far from here still remain pure, beyond the reach of the black fog. I do not know if these stories are true or where these places might be, but 'tis possible we shall find them and such help as they may afford on our journey." Shaka tied one of the backpacks closed. The other was almost ready as well.

"You must trust that I know the ways of the woods," Shaka continued. "I know them as well as the birds and the beasts, and few can make such a claim. We shall take Tak and Gallia—and I have a weapon to protect us." She motioned toward the near side of the fireplace to what appeared to be a musical string instrument with a neck that turned into a crossbow. Laney gave Shaka a puzzled look, but then Shaka moved aside the lute, breaking the illusion and revealing a marvelously crafted crossbow. Intricate gold inlays adorned the crossbow's wooden stock, and the weapon had an age and majesty of a precious heirloom.

Shaka picked up a quiver of arrows, all with black feathers. She inspected the shafts, each one decorated with a thin band of fine, colored thread—some golden yellow, others blue, others purple. Shaka hesitated a moment and then retrieved, from the far side of the room behind a leather-strapped chest, another arrow with black feathers. Unlike the others, it had a band of crimson thread decorating the shaft. Shaka looked at it, paused a moment as if lost in thought, and then put it into her quiver.

"These arrows are unlike any crafted from the days of old," she said. "They are guided not only by the aim of the archer but by the power of their makers from long ago. Gold is Protection, azure is Destiny, and violet is Wrath—choose the right arrow, and the aim is always true." Shaka pulled up a handful of the arrows so that Laney could see the different colors on the shafts.

"What's the red one?" Laney asked.

"The crimson arrow," said Shaka, "—the arrow of Sacrifice. There is only one crimson arrow. If the stories hold true, this arrow brings victory, but the price is high. The tales of old claim that whoever uses the crimson arrow shall not survive. But I do not know. This arrow has not been used since before any person now living came into this world." Shaka put the crimson arrow back into the quiver. "'Tis not wise to tempt the fates, but if the need arises, I shall use the crimson arrow.

"Now we need to hurry, or we shall lose the best part of the day," Shaka continued. "The syzygy shall not wait. The packs are ready, but you are not."

Laney made no reply.

"You must wear one of my crystals to channel your powers—must choose the right one." Shaka paced back and forth. "Something strong," she muttered, "strong enough for a sorceress!" She reached to the mantel and retrieved an ornate wooden box, bringing it back to the table. When she lifted its lid, Laney could see quartz-like crystals of various shapes, sizes, and colors—all necklaces with woven black string.

"My crystals have not the power of the great stones Sarazal of the East and Agashore of the West, but they will aid us on our journey. For a new bearer, they are especially potent once you learn how to use their energy. Each has the ability to strengthen a power of the person who wears it." She held them up one at a time. "This rose crystal fans the flame of bravery. The canary crystal hardens the will so that no task is too difficult to overcome. And this one that looks like the sky on a stormy day provides strength when most needed."

"Why don't you wear them all?" asked Laney.

Shaka raised an eyebrow. "Their magic must not interfere with one another," she explained. "A crystal must be worn alone. I wear the azure crystal of second sight. It guides my dreams and gives me faith in what lies ahead."

Shaka put back the crystal she had been holding and retrieved instead an orange-red stone that sparkled from within. A braid of silver-like metal entwined the gem, accenting its beauty. "This one," she declared. "There is no other like it —the Sun Stone. It will sharpen your senses and guide your spirit when the need is most great. Perchance it shall help you find your lost memories—we shall see. It shall grow in power as the syzygy approaches. Wear it under your garments against your skin, and it will serve you well. Of all the crystals and stones, this one alone has a second power—if tales be true. Neither this gem nor the person who wears it shall ever be taken by force. I have never tested that claim, but we shall see. I now give it to you. I paid a high price to acquire it—may it serve you well." She placed the necklace over Laney's head, and Laney tucked it beneath her shirt without remembering to say "Thank you."—but Shaka, very much focused on last-minute preparations, seemed not to notice as she turned her attention now to weaponry.

"You have no sword, not even a knife. Which do you prefer?" she asked.

"I don't know," replied Laney. "I don't know how to use them."

"Very well," said Shaka, "I shall carry a blade for us both—and my crossbow." She went into the back room of the cottage and returned with a hunting knife.

"Behold—the Blade of Kramariton!" Shaka unsheathed the blade, revealing its craftsmanship. Two birds with extraordinary plumage graced the flat while the handle featured a bird head fashioned to please the hand as well as the eye. "'Twas my father's, and then passed on to me. 'Tis a fitting choice for our journey." She sheathed the blade and fastened it to her belt.

Next Shaka retrieved two hooded cloaks from pegs on the wall near the door. She handed one to Laney. "You shall need this," she said. "Your garments are strange to me, but this cloak shall keep you warm like no other. 'Tis light as a dusting of snow, but at night it shall protect you like the warmth of the sun."

Laney marveled at the texture of the cloak. "I can hardly feel it," she said.

"'Tis the finest of wool and the best of the master weavers."

"Wool?" asked Laney in disbelief. "From a sheep?"

Shaka laughed. "Not sheep—rabbits!" She continued to chuckle as she readied for the trip. Then she said to Laney, "You shall need a staff—to steady your feet, and perhaps more. Come—choose wisely." She led Laney to a corner where several carved sticks leaned against the wall. Laney had never used a walking stick, and her inclination was to simply take the one in front. But when she reached toward the pile, she found herself pushing the nearest ones aside. One behind began to fall, and she caught it as it headed toward the floor.

"That is the one," said Shaka.

Laney held the stick a moment and then tested it against the floor, pleased that it felt light but strong. But she had no desire to journey through the woods. "Is there another way?" she asked.

"The woods are all around us," said Shaka. "Shall you stay here alone?"

Laney bowed her head a moment, and then lifted her gaze to meet Shaka's. "I'm scared."

Shaka nodded. "Your answers lie in the clearing. For surely the ice and snow that fell upon you so mightily at my door did not snatch your memory. No, 'twas the magic of the West Woods. You came from there, where few dare to venture, and none escape unscathed. Your only cure is to find the clearing. Unless you come with me, you shall never know your past."

Nevanna and Divanna

"Come now. We must get started," said Shaka. She put on the larger of the two packs and then helped Laney put on the other. Then Shaka slung her quiver across her shoulder and grabbed her crossbow and a walking stick.

With their cloaks secured, they both stepped outside. Shaka whistled to Tak and Gallia, and the dogs bounded toward her.

Laney squinted in the bright sunlight, but she welcomed the crisp, fresh air.

"This is Winterfylleth," said Shaka, "the start of the winter season. We shall have snow in the days ahead, but the trees catch much of it. What has already fallen through shall not last. See how it glistens? The sun makes it weep, and the wind whisks away the tears." Indeed, Laney could see that the snow shimmered like diamonds, so much so that it hurt her eyes to look upon it. Then Shaka raised her voice as if issuing a command to legions of followers. "Follow me!" she bellowed, and she plunged ahead with both dogs beside her. Laney took one last look over her shoulder at the cabin, and then followed after Shaka.

"Tak—look after Laney," Shaka commanded one of the dogs, "and no chasing rabbits!"

And so their journey began as they left comforts behind and headed west toward the heart of the forest. They quickly struck a narrow dirt path and followed it winding through the trees.

Sights, sounds, and smells aroused Laney's senses as if she were now truly awake for the first time—the feel and sound of crunching snow, the shimmering of sunlight, the slap of the cold breeze, the swirling of pine scent in the air. It all came with a ring of familiarity, yet each experience felt like the first, a moment to savor, like tasting a forgotten favorite food.

"You came from these woods," Shaka remarked, "a treacherous journey no doubt. Perchance you shall remember some of where we walk, though the West Woods has many paths, and they shift like sands in the desert. Many a woodsman has become lost, never to return. But paths or not, I shall lead us where we must go, and Tak and Gallia shall then lead us home—they have that sense about them. When our quest is fulfilled and the evil that harnesses the spirit of the wolves is no more, harmony shall return to the West Woods, and we shall return to Tarzetta Trail."

"That is the prophecy?" asked Laney.

"When Autumn's breeze gives way to snow,
And dreams portend a coming foe,
And in your heart you truly know,
Look to the midday sun.
When Moon begins a parting smile,
Coyly chasing all the while
Golden goddess down her aisle,
The magic has begun.
A sorceress from westward land
Will blindly come to lend a hand
And two brave souls shall make a stand,
The day of the darkening sun."

Shaka's voice lingered on the last word, and then she looked keenly at Laney. "There is much more to it than that, of course—the 'Song of Tarzetta' as handed down from generation to generation. But this much I know—I am a brave soul, one of the two. I have known it always, even before I heard the song as a little girl. Other girls dream of family and days of plenty—not I. My thoughts are ever with the wolves—in my dreams and waking hours, for as long as I can remember. And now the wolves become more bold and venture ever nearer to my home. Your coming is not by chance—you shall see."

Laney sighed, that one breath conveying all her doubts and fears.

The sun climbed high behind them, and presently Shaka stopped and lay down her pack. "Here we shall take a brief rest," she said. "Let us now eat to keep up our strength. We have made a good start."

Laney removed her pack, but before she could sit down upon it, Shaka opened it and retrieved some carefully wrapped dried fruits and nuts.

"You have done well today," she said as she shared the snack with Laney. Laney did not recognize any of the food and wondered whether it was something she had forgotten, or something new to her. The yellow and orange strips of fruit smelled inviting. She tasted a piece and smiled as the sweetness rolled across her tongue.

"The forest is calm today," observed Shaka.

"You mean the wind?" asked Laney.

"No, the trees," said Shaka as she motioned toward all that surrounded them. "The roots beneath our feet are never from a single tree. One tree's roots touches another and another, in an ever widening circle throughout the vastness of the forest. Each tree feels all that affects any other—harm one and you harm them all. This forest is old, and it never forgets. Its memory of woodsmen felling trees to clear trails and build homes is as fresh as spring blooms. This forest cares not for any who walk on two legs."

Laney had never thought of trees that way, and didn't know what to make of that, except she knew the forest made her uneasy. But before she could ponder that at any length, Shaka stood and motioned for her and the dogs to resume their journey.

Tak walked beside Laney, and she sensed that he was indeed looking after her. He sometimes rubbed up against her hip and wagged his tail.

Time passed with Shaka telling Laney family stories about growing up in the woods, how she had been taught her skills and what Laney would do well to learn. Laney for her part had not much to say and was content to simply listen.

The sky remained clear, but the wind picked up out of the west. Though the forest blocked much of its force, gusts weaved their way through the trees and along the path. Laney put her head down and leaned forward. She became lost in thought as she wondered what she might be doing now if she hadn't lost her memory.

Overhead the canopy swayed, buffeted by the winds. Tak barked twice, his nose pointed to the sky. Laney looked up—too late. A dead branch targeted her as if it had a will to strike.

The branch hit with such force that it shattered, yet Laney stood unharmed. Shaka had met the branch with her walking stick, and the dead wood was no match for her skill.

Laney turned to Shaka with a look of shock and wonder.

"I can teach you," said Shaka. "Until your powers return, you must learn to protect yourself as I do."

Tak nudged Laney's leg with his face.

"You knew!" she said.

"When Tak senses danger, you must heed his warnings," said Shaka. "When he barks twice, danger is coming as sure as thunder follows the flash."

"I'll remember that." Laney gave a respectful nod to Tak, and petted his massive shoulder, and he acknowledged her with a wag of his tail.

Shaka continued to lead as quickly as Laney could follow, and when the pace began to slow, Shaka called for a halt. They ate a ration of provisions from Shaka's pack, but all too soon they resumed their trek. Laney's feet, legs, and back ached, and she felt energy draining from her body.

The trail became more difficult as the forest tried to reclaim it. Trees encroached on either side, their low-lying branches crossing over the path, while seedlings and saplings had sprung up laying claim to the wider parts of the trail.

The day wore on, and the westering sun flitting in and out of the trees shone upon Laney's face. She squinted as she looked into the distance—nothing but trees. But suddenly Tak growled and barked twice. Shaka stopped and held up a hand. She turned her head this way and that, sniffing the air, and then in an instant fitted an arrow in her crossbow. "You there! Show yourself!" Shaka commanded. "And over there!" she said, turning. "Speak quickly friend or foe ere I decide for myself!"

Laney held her breath.

"Attack an old woman minding her own business?—indeed *you* are a foe!" came a crackling reply from behind a tree.

"Show us no harm, and you have naught to fear," Shaka said as she lowered her crossbow, but kept her finger on the trigger.

A face peeked from behind one of the trees, and then two women stepped out into the open. So similar were they that certainly they were twins. Yet more striking than their similarity was their appearance, for both displayed ravages of time and toil beyond compare: cascades of wrinkles, black blotches of rot, the gummy ruins of missing teeth. Each wore a tattered black cape with black garments beneath.

Tak and Gallia growled but stood fast.

"We are Nevanna . . . and Divanna," they said, one after the other. Together they approached Shaka.

Laney felt a chill go down her spine. She put a hand on Tak's shoulder.

"What business have you in the West Woods so far from comforts and care?" asked Shaka, as she looked the women over from head to toe.

"We seek roots and barks, and though we are old, we need no comforts and care," said Nevanna. Divanna nodded in agreement.

. . . both displayed ravages of time and toil beyond compare.

"Roots and barks under cover of snow?" Shaka questioned.

"The trees sleep under the snow, and only a fool would disturb them otherwise," replied Divanna. "Even with our magic we must be careful in the West Woods."

"Magic?" said Laney, surprised by her own boldness and curiosity.

"Of course," replied Divanna. "How else might we be here?"

Nevanna stepped closer and eyed Laney. "You are a curious one," she said. "You do not belong here." The woman licked her wrinkled lips and wiped away the drool.

Now both women focused their attention on Laney. "Ask us a question," they said in unison.

The odor of rotten breath and the foul spittle from each word nearly overwhelmed Laney, yet she found herself asking, "Where is my home?"

Nevanna and Divanna shared a toothless smile, and Laney sensed she had just given more information than she would receive.

"Shall we take you there?" asked Nevanna.

"Out of the woods, far away," said Divanna.

Laney looked at Shaka, who shook her head.

"What have you to trade . . ." asked Divanna.

". . . for this?" said Nevanna, turning to Shaka, and she held aloft a necklace with a translucent stone the color of maple syrup. The stone caught the light, and Laney could see something inside . . . a spider!

"You shall need this," said Nevanna to Shaka.

"'Twill keep you safe from traps, and webs, and spiders," claimed Divanna.

"Big spiders!" Nevanna added as she stuck her knobby hand toward Shaka, wiggling her fingers like spider legs.

Then Nevanna tossed back her scraggly hair and revealed . . . spiders! All along her scrawny neck they appeared to march. A shiny hoop earring, shimmering in the breeze, framed the largest spider, as if holding it captive.

Just ink, thought Laney, but the dangling hoop caught a sliver of sunlight that seemed to bring the one spider to life.

As Laney looked on, Shaka appeared frozen, staring. But then Tak growled and sprang toward Nevanna, and the old woman jumped back with surprising agility, her face flushed with anger.

"Nasty creature!" she exclaimed as she cowered toward her sister, who whispered something into her ear.

"Tasty . . . yes . . . give us one of the dogs," said Nevanna, "and this shall keep you safe." She again held the necklace out toward Shaka.

But the mesmerizing spell of the twirling earring had been broken, and Shaka made no effort to hide her contempt. "I have no need for your charms and trinkets," she sneered.

"Give and take," said Divanna. "Those who brave the West Woods must help one another. What have you to share?"

"We have nothing save what we need," snapped Shaka.

Then Nevanna's eyes fell upon the handle of Shaka's blade, and she knew it at once. "The Blade of Kramariton!" Nevanna exclaimed. "One of my kinsmen bore that blade, a treasure beyond compare. They say he fell from a cliff, but his hand was severed and his fingers pried from the grip. 'Twas no accident!"

"I know not the tale you tell," said Shaka. "My father gave me this blade, and my father was an honorable man."

"A convenient excuse to take what is not yours," retorted Divanna.

"My kinsman's blood is on the hands of any who would draw this blade, save the rightful owner," declared Nevanna. "Give it to me now lest it betray you when you need it most."

"This blade has served me well," replied Shaka, "and I chose it for this journey. I shall not surrender it now."

Nevanna's face twitched and flushed with rage. She shook her fist as she eyed Shaka's crossbow.

Meanwhile, Divanna turned to Laney again. "What is this?" she asked as she reached her hideous fingers toward the black string of Laney's necklace. Laney instinctively swatted Divanna's hand, and the woman lurched back as if stung by a bee. Laney then grasped where the crystal lay hidden, and Nevanna and Divanna raised their hands as if to ward off a blow.

"Dare not touch the Sorceress from the West," Shaka commanded, "lest she turn you into a mole!" And such was the wrath in her voice and the unknown threat beneath Laney's hand that both women cringed and trembled.

"We mean no harm," said Divanna, while Nevanna mumbled and wrapped her cape around her body.

"Begone!" yelled Shaka, and she raised her crossbow.

Nevanna and Divanna backed away.

Gallia and Tak both growled, ready for any command from Shaka.

The women sneered in return. "You shall see," said Divanna. "We offer what you need. Dark times await!"

Then quick as cats the women reached inside their capes—Nevanna flung her hands up into the air while Divanna flung hers toward the ground—and in a blinding flash of light and billow of smoke, they were gone.

"Wow!" said Laney when the smoke cleared. "Was that magic?"

"Just tricks—nothing more," Shaka scoffed.

"They looked like witches!" said Laney.

"Fake magicians," Shaka replied, "and cheats, I have no doubt—peddling cures for spiders—in winter, no less.

Laney frowned. She had a bad feeling about those women—and their spiders.

The Allure of Dalida

Shadows stretched behind them as they followed the sun westward. "Soon we shall seek shelter for the night," Shaka said. "We dare not travel in the dark."

"Is there a place to stay?" asked Laney.

Shaka laughed. "Not that kind of shelter—but we shall see. My knowledge of the woods shall keep us safe and warm enough for the night." She stepped off the path and headed into the maze of trees.

Laney was reluctant to leave the trail, but she welcomed an end to the day's journey. Her first steps off the path plunged downward along rough terrain tangled with vines and fallen branches, and within no time, all signs of the trail disappeared. Shaka led them into a valley and along the bottom of a ridge, and they came to a depression in the hillside.

Shaka nodded, a hint of a smile on her face. "This will do. 'Tis shelter from the wind, and I shall build a fire."

They lay their packs down against the earthen wall. "Rest 'til I return," said Shaka. She motioned for Gallia to come with her.

Laney had no desire for anything but rest. She sat on her pack, and Tak lay down beside her.

"You're looking out for me, aren't you?" said Laney.

Tak rested his chin on her leg and looked into her eyes.

"Why can't I remember?" she said, running her hands through his thick fur.

As Laney sat with Tak, the trees began to fade into the growing darkness. Then, almost without a sound, Shaka and Gallia reappeared. Shaka dumped an armful of sticks and began the painstaking task of building a fire. She started the flame with a tinderbox she retrieved from her pack, and then nursed it along until the twigs began to burn. Soon the flickering grew into a crackling blaze.

"So, you can live off of sticks and dirt and bugs," Laney teased, shaking her head. She knew she belonged elsewhere.

"Bugs?" said Shaka.

"You know, little crawly things on the ground—bugs."

"Humph—there are no little crawly things in winter," said Shaka, "but I can build a fire with sticks, and I do not mind getting my hands dirty. I know how to hunt and gather, and I have enough sense to take what I need when I venture out." Shaka reached into Laney's pack and retrieved dried fruit and nuts for their evening meal.

"You did well today," said Shaka.

Laney leaned toward the dancing flames, delighted by the warmth. "I don't belong here. What are you going to do with me when you figure out I'm not a sorceress?"

"When the time comes, we shall both see who you are and what you can do. I shall accept whatever that may be. You have made no promise to me."

"I follow you because—what else can I do?"

"We shall see." Shaka nodded.

They sat in silence for a while, until Laney's curiosity stirred. "What do you know about these woods?"

"More than most," replied Shaka, "but there is much to know, for the history of the West Woods goes back beyond reckoning. I shall tell you a story as my mother told it to me, and as her mother to her. It is but a small part of a great tale that begins in times long gone and joins other tales, all with an end that has not yet been written."

And so she began: "Long ago two villages, Buroakville and Peltston, thrived deep in the West Woods. Buroakville boasted the finest craftsmen in all the land, and Peltston laid claim to the largest fur trade in the West Woods and beyond. Traders and merchants came from faraway lands, and villagers enjoyed prosperity beyond the dreams of most. In celebration of their success, the master artists and craftsmen erected a great stone arch to grace the eastern border where the two villages met. When the great arch stood complete, it was indeed a wonder to behold. Such was its beauty that many declared it must be magical. Visitors claimed that simply by passing beneath the arch, their spirit would soar to such heights that they would burst into song.

"In the cold days of winter, visits from traders would all but cease. But one winter, on the least likely of days, the sun shone like summer. Villagers opened their doors in joy as icicles dripped like rain, and snow melted into endless pools. On that day someone new passed through the arch, and as she stepped foot on the other side, a song flowed from her lips the likes of which no one had ever heard. So sweet was the music that those nearby rushed toward it to see how such sounds might be. A crowd gathered, and word quickly spread about the mysterious traveler. Her name, she said, was Dalida, though she offered no clue from whence she came. She brought with her a fruit of the gods, she claimed—red as an apple but thrice the size, and inside a thousand drops of luscious sweetness as rich as honey and as red as the finest rubies in the land. One taste of the fruit was as alluring as her song, and soon everyone wanted to trade for this fruit of the gods. Timor and Graigon, the leaders of Buroakville and Peltston, came to greet Dalida, and both men were smitten. Timor had no wife, and so fancied that Dalida would be his. Graigon had a wife of many years, but her virtues did not compare—loyalty and devotion paled before the mystery and beauty of Dalida. When Dalida pulled off her cloak that warm winter day and tossed back her hair, none could turn away. For in addition to bare shoulders, her scant top revealed—a tiger! Its paws rested upon the upper curve of each breast, its mouth agape in the center. As Dalida's chest rose and fell with each breath, the tiger moved as if it were alive. Its eyes followed anyone so bold as to look, and with paws stretched outward, the tiger crouched—waiting.

"Timor and Graigon entreated Dalida to stay, and she accepted both invitations. Over the following weeks, Dalida stayed with first one and then the other, and then back and forth again. She would leave on a whim, and return days later unannounced, and each time her host would become more desperate to keep her company. Timor and Graigon showered her with gifts, each trying to outdo the other, and neither could contain his jealousy.

"What happened next is unclear, except we know that Dalida disappeared, and Graigon and Timor fell victim to their faults and each other's wrath. In the end both villages burned, and Graigon and Timor perished. The villagers who survived became scattered. No more traders came to buy and sell wares, and the once peaceful and prosperous land fell into decay. For where good no longer thrives, evil feels welcome.

"Not long after the fall of Buroakville and Pelston, the black fog came from the Northwest Mountains. It rolled and tumbled through the forest, bringing with it a putrid smell and a chill of death. Ever since, the black fog comes and goes without warning, like a sudden storm. And when it comes, it brings the wolves.

"After the black fog came to the West Woods, no one dared to venture to the lost villages—at least not anyone who ever returned. If stories be true, the great arch still stands, but no longer does it lift the spirits of travelers. Whether the evil of the forest seeped into its wondrous carvings or a spell became cast upon it, no one can say. But stories handed down from father to son and mother to daughter claim that after the coming of the black fog, anyone passing beneath the great arch would disappear—some say carried by magic or spirits to another time and place. How much truth is in these stories, I do not know, but maybe 'tis how a sorceress could come and go. Perchance you came through this arch, and the power that delivered you took away your memory. Magic and spells are not to be meddled with lightly."

Shaka stood and took a deep breath. "There is much more to this story, but it must wait for the light of day." She tilted her head back toward the stars, and then lowered her gaze toward Laney. "We journey now in the land of prophecy. Soon enough you shall be put to the test, and then we shall see."

Zelfore

Laney awoke to a crisp breeze and the smell of dog breath—Tak lay beside her, studying her face and then wagging his tail as she stirred and squinted in the morning sun.

She sat up and looked past Tak to where Shaka appeared to be fighting an invisible opponent. Shaka spun around twirling her walking stick and then thrust it forward, flipped it end over end, and then brought it back down beside her. She took a few deep breaths, and nodded toward Laney.

"Come. I shall teach you."

Laney shook her head, but Shaka would have her way.

"Do not hold it at the end—hold it as I do," Shaka said as she gripped her stick with hands shoulder-width apart, closer to the middle. "Now watch my eyes. You can read much from the eyes—fear, anger, and the aim of the next blow."

She led Laney through a series of continuous motions with her stick. "Be both gentle as a breeze and strong as a gale," she said, "and strike like thunder."

She swung at Laney's stick, and the blow landed like a sledgehammer, its force vibrating through Laney's body.

Shaka smiled. "Lightning and thunder—you will learn. Again, do as I do with your stick, and I shall tell you when to strike."

Laney tried several times, and gradually her blows gained strength against Shaka's seemingly immovable stick.

"There is fire in your eyes. This is good! Now strike with the point, like so . . ." And with a single move Shaka scooped Laney's stick out of the way and thrust the tip of her weapon toward Laney's chest. Then she stepped back and waited for Laney to attack.

"No," Shaka scolded as Laney clumsily shoved her stick toward Shaka. "Your whole body and spirit must be behind your thrust. Your arms alone will not fend off the fury of a charging wolf. Do it again!"

Laney struggled to get her body to move the way Shaka wanted. After several attempts she started to get the hang of it, and finally Shaka smiled. "You learn quickly," she said. "'Tis more difficult than it seems. But that is enough for your first lesson. Remember what you have learned, and tomorrow I shall show you more."

Laney nodded as she caught her breath.

They readied themselves and their packs, and soon they were back on their feet heading in a westerly direction. Though Laney had lagged behind most of the previous day, a good night's sleep fueled her curiosity, and she caught up with Shaka. "Who is the Sorceress from the West?" she asked.

Shaka gave no answer at first, but presently she spoke: "The Sorceress from the West is a mystery even to the wise. None who live this day can claim to know her, yet her coming has been foretold. Some say the Sorceress can ride the waves of time and travel to and from other worlds, and that she might appear or disappear at any time. Others claim that the true Sorceress will be able to command the elements of nature—a flood, an avalanche, maybe even command the mountains to let loose their fire and ash. The prophecy declares that the Sorceress shall arrive in the time leading up to a syzygy, and the power of the Sorceress and the ancient arrows shall prevail against the evil of the West Woods. I am the keeper of the arrows, and you have arrived at the time foretold."

"You said the Sorceress is blind?"

"According to the prophecy," Shaka responded, "but nothing is known about how or why, or even what is meant by 'blind'. A prophecy can be like a riddle.

Someone who can see may be blind to a great many things—especially someone with no memory."

"Tell me more about the West Woods," said Laney, changing the subject. "You didn't finish your story yesterday."

"The tale goes on to this day," said Shaka in a softer tone, "but the part that begins where I left off is filled with sorrow. I shall tell it only briefly so as not to dampen our spirits.

"After the passing of Graigon and Timor and the coming of the black fog, much of the West Woods fell into decay. Wolves came to rule, and the howls of the packs spread from the time of the moon through the time of the sun. The wolves killed beyond their need for food, leaving deer to rot on the forest floor.

"But the forest endured. Rain and snow and wind work their magic, and the black fog does not last—for now. But it comes without warning, and it is spreading.

"For a time, no one dared to venture more than a day's journey into the West Woods, and even Tarzetta Trail ceased to be traveled by any but the few who guarded its borders. By the time brave men and women once again heeded the call of the forest, they discovered that beyond the new growth, the trails they knew had disappeared—how that came to pass, no one could say. Nonetheless, those who dreamt of a bountiful forest resolved to make new trails. They felled the trees that stood in their way, and they brought hunters with them to protect against the wolves.

"These new trails started where the paths of old once lay, but the land proved difficult and unpredictable, with cliffs and ravines, streams and rivers where none had been known before. Rocky cliffs let loose boulders, and spring storms toppled trees. And the wolves came, pack after pack. Often the black fog would accompany them, and no man or woman could face the terror of the two. The black fog they say felt like an army of ghosts coming for battle. After a time, all work on the trails became abandoned, including the extension of Tarzetta Trail.

"The West Woods shall never be tamed by trails. Its heart shall be forever dark until the prophecy is fulfilled. The black fog does not come into what we call the new growth, the easternmost part of the West Woods that I call my home, but lone wolves and small packs sometimes do, and they are becoming more bold. If the prophecy is not fulfilled, dark times await. I see it in my dreams. If left unchallenged, the power of the fog shall spread, and what then shall become of the West Woods and beyond? No one can say."

"So to get to the clearing, we're going toward the black fog and wolves—alone!"

"Two travelers with dogs shall not attract the attention of whatever commands the wolves and the black fog, at least not until we near the clearing," Shaka said. "We are safer without more companions. Had we all the warriors and weapons within seven days' travel, still we would be no match for the full force of the wolves. Their numbers are beyond counting, and with the black fog, they are terrible. We shall journey alone, unnoticed, and that will be best."

"But what happens when we get there?"

"I have the weapon of the prophecy to protect us," said Shaka. "The power of the arrows is great indeed, and they were fashioned of old for just such a purpose. Wolves and black fog . . . and something more. There is something that drives them both, and when we get to the clearing we shall discover what that might be. If the power that lays hold over these woods presents itself when we get to the clearing, I shall be ready. The arrows will aim true, black fog or not, and they will bring fear to even the most fearless." And then Shaka added, "You shall play a role, Laney, though what that may be, I cannot say. Sometimes 'tis better to know that a deed will get done than to know how it will happen."

After a brief rest, Shaka led them at a brisk pace due west. As luck would have it, they chanced upon a trail heading in their direction. Laney felt relieved, but Shaka studied the ground with concern.

"Someone walks this path," she said. "Not far ahead."

Laney bent down to look at the clues that Shaka had found, but all she saw were patches of undisturbed snow and leaves.

Shaka doubled her pace, but Laney kept up. The trail weaved its way through the trees such that they could never see more than a short distance ahead. Suddenly Shaka stopped.

"Whoever we follow, their trail ends here," she said as she studied the ground. "The signs all disappear." She looked about and then upward as if she wondered whether their mysterious stranger had sprouted wings. She sniffed the air. "There is a smell like turpentine hiding among the pines," she said.

"Hiding? No, napping until you came this way," huffed a voice from beside the path, "and I smelled the four of you back when your shadows led the way."

Then just off the path, what appeared to be nothing more than a mound of earth and leaves rose up, and with a twirl revealed itself—a man cloaked in earthen-colored attire with a hat to match and a beard like fine winter brush flecked with snow. He wore heavy boots and an oversized cloak that looked as if its threads were interwoven with dirt and leaves.

"I like to say 'well met' when I greet travelers on the paths of the West Woods, but I am not so sure. I do not meet many in these times, and some are none too friendly. Are you friendly?"

Shaka's hand reached for her knife, but she did not draw the blade. "If we have disturbed your peace, then accept my apology," she said, "but you are new and mysterious to us. We mean you no harm."

"Well spoken, but tell me why you are here, and then I shall judge whether you mean me no harm." The man spoke with a firm, but not unpleasant, voice.

"I am Shaka, the Guardian of Tarzetta Trail, and my companion is called Laney. We are passing through this land on a journey westward."

"If you are the Guardian of Tarzetta Trail, then you are far from home. What urgent matter brings you so deep into these woods?" He spoke as if he were a father questioning an errant child.

"I think you know, or you would not ask so directly," replied Shaka. "These times and the coming of the syzygy are no secret from one who knows the West Woods. Who are you and what brings you here?"

The man laughed. "Yes, I know why you travel, and I know a bit more as well. I am Zelfore, and I have lived long and traveled far."

"I too have travelled far, but I have never met the likes of you," Shaka replied.

"I could say as much about the four of you," said Zelfore. "Are we not each one of a kind?"

Shaka made no reply, and Zelfore continued, "So you seek to change the West Woods, restore it to its former glory. Not everyone will welcome such change. There are those who prefer that it remain a place where fear keeps people away. If you meet any such man or creature, beware! Not every hand is a helping hand."

"What about your hand?" said Shaka, still sizing up Zelfore.

"My hand has all its fingers," said Zelfore as he waved them in front of his face, "which means I have not tried to take what is not mine. That is how you lose fingers, or maybe an entire hand.

"Trust your heart," Zelfore continued, "but also your head. Alone either can easily be deceived, but together they make quite a pair. You will have hard choices to make in the days ahead, and your will shall be put to the test. A prophecy does not fulfill itself, and some prophesies will never come to pass. For how can we truly know what is a prophecy and what is simply the hopes and dreams of a people put into song? We cannot. And sometimes the hopes and dreams come true while the prophecy remains unfulfilled."

"The prophecy is real," said Shaka.

"Perhaps," said Zelfore, "but no matter. It will come to pass only by deeds, and not by words of the wise or anyone else. If the deeds fail, what then? Those deeds will be forgotten, but your prophecy will remain. How many deeds came before yours? No one can say. Songs do not celebrate deeds that fall short."

And then Zelfore turned his gaze from Shaka to Laney. "You, silent one, what have you to say?"

"Hi." Laney didn't want to say anything, but didn't want to be rude.

"Hmmm—is that all?"

Caught off guard by the brusk response, Laney asked the first question that popped into her head. "Are you one of the wise?"

Zelfore laughed again. "Anyone who is truly wise realizes he knows very little. I know more than a little, so perhaps I am not so wise. What about you? Are you wise?"

"I know nothing more than the past few days," Laney replied.

"Few days?" Zelfore exclaimed with surprise. "That is a long time indeed, longer than I can imagine. For me, the only day that happens is today. There is no yesterday, only today gone by. And there is no tomorrow—only today yet to be. The present is all that matters, and it matters forever, for it is all there is and all there ever will be. I cannot live in tomorrow or yesterday, nor can the sun and the moon, who constantly journey to join today. 'Tis only an illusion that the days are moving! I have been here since the dawn of today, and I shall be here through its eternity. But in this day, I have learned much, and if you wish you may ask me a question—and then you may judge for yourself whether I am indeed one of the wise."

"Where is my home?" Laney asked, hoping for a better answer than she got from the magician twins.

Zelfore stood silent for a moment. "Some people know their home because they never leave," he finally said, "and others know it only when they return. You are the latter. I cannot tell you how to get there, only that the more you journey, the more you will understand."

Laney frowned. She wanted to understand the wisdom in these words, but they felt hollow.

"The shadows grow long," said Shaka to Zelfore, "and soon we must seek shelter. What might we find up ahead?"

"Trees, glorious trees—but also a cave. Head into the valley, and follow the stream. When it bends south, you shall come upon a great rock. There the cave shall be revealed."

"Will you not show us the way?" asked Shaka. "Do you not seek shelter yourself?"

"I need no such shelter," said Zelfore, "and my way is elsewhere. Hurry along or you will not find your cave before dark. I shall take a moment for rest and reflection before I continue with my day." And with that said, Zelfore twirled around and, folding his arms and legs and tucking his head, once again disappeared into the landscape as nothing more than a mound at the base of a tree. Tak barked, and Shaka released her grip from the handle of her knife. She kept her eye on the mound as she started forward along the path, motioning Laney and the dogs to follow.

Heeding Zelfore's advice, Shaka led them off the trail and into the valley. The terrain rolled gently down at first, and then more steeply, forcing Laney to grab hold of trunks and branches to keep from falling. But this valley was not deep, and soon they neared the bottom. The stream lay smooth and frozen before them, and they followed it winding through the hills. Then true to Zelfore's word, after a sharp bend to the south, they found themselves standing before a rock that towered above their heads. They marveled at how it came to be there, but they had more pressing concerns—no cave appeared in any direction.

"I sensed no deception in Zelfore's voice," Shaka said. "I must get to the top of this rock to see what I might see."

Shaka's hands clutched the rough surface, and with much effort she climbed to the top.

She stood upon the rock and looked in all directions. To the west the land rose as an almost sheer cliff to a height well above that of the rock, and then jutted inward. With the westering sun, deep shadows lay across the face of the cliff.

"I see our cave," Shaka declared, "but getting there shall not be easy."

"I see our cave," Shaka declared, "but getting there shall not be easy. We must hurry if we hope to arrive before dark."

They had to backtrack to leave the valley, but eventually they found themselves at the top of the slope leading to the cave. They descended carefully, but the ledge at the base proved to be wide—they could have slept comfortably outside the cave without being near the edge of the cliff.

"Are there bears maybe?" Laney asked, more curious than concerned.

"I see no signs," said Shaka. "They have not sought sleep for the winter, and their numbers are few."

With the failing light and the cave opening facing east, the inside proved to be impenetrably dark. They worked their way into the depths of the cave where the relative warmth of the damp interior proved a welcome change from the freezing wind. The tunnel narrowed at first, but then the surrounding walls gave way, and Shaka and Laney could tell by the change in the air and the echo of their footsteps that they had entered a vast cavern.

"Here we shall sleep," said Shaka. "We must not wander farther in and chance losing our way out. Tak and Gallia have a keen nose and a sense for direction, but I do not trust this cave. We shall be warm and dry for the night. Tak and Gallia shall help me keep watch."

Fumbling in the dark, Laney and Shaka found provisions for themselves and the dogs, and after a quick bite to eat, they all settled in for the night. Laney emptied her pack of the softer items and spread them out to lie upon. She used the mostly empty pack as a pillow. Soon the only sound she could hear was the soft breathing of her companions, and a drip-drip-drip coming from somewhere in the cavern. Laney had no recollection of water making such a sound, yet somehow it seemed familiar.

She pretended to be lying in a comfortable room, imagining four walls around her as she listened to the drip-drip-drip. But something about this cave made her uneasy—more than uneasy—and she worried that soon she'd find out why.

The Cave

In the blackness of the cave, no one saw the spider. Its finger-like legs moved silently ever closer to Shaka, and then it stepped onto her arm. So tired was Shaka, that half asleep she reached to scratch an itch, and the spider's fangs found her hand.

The pain shot into her hand so suddenly that in an instant she reacted, hurling the spider into the air.

"What's wrong?" said Laney, her voice hoarse from sleep.

The dogs offered an ominous growl.

"Spiders the size of bullfrogs!" exclaimed Shaka. "Our good fortune is naught—we cannot stay the night."

But just then a faint glow came from a passage at the far side of the chamber. Laney held her breath, and Shaka readied an arrow. Her hand shook from the pain and the poison working its way up her arm, but she kept her aim as best she could.

The glow transformed into a point of light—a torch carried toward them. Moments later the flame shone upon a man of great girth, but small stature. Had Tak advanced toward the man, the two of them would have seen eye to eye. The man's nose protruded from beneath a gray hood, and the flame from the torch made his eyes twinkle. Boots the size of snowshoes peeked past the bottom of his dusty cloak. In one hand he held the torch. In the other he wielded an axe.

His beard wagged as he bellowed, "Who dares trespass? Speak swiftly lest you arouse my wrath!" He glared at the travelers and raised his axe with such speed and ease that no doubt he could have thrown it like a knife.

"I am Odenzod, son of Oraszod, of the great house Alrondan."

"I am Shaka, and these are my companions. We came seeking shelter and nothing else. We knew not that any laid claim to this land."

The man pointed his torch forward to get a better look. "I am Odenzod, son of Oraszod, of the great house Alrondan. What led you here where no one dares to come?"

"Neither fortune nor fate, but one who calls himself Zelfore," Shaka replied.

"Zelfore!" exclaimed the stout man, and he lowered his axe. "These are treacherous times, but the coming of Zelfore is great news indeed. Tell me what he spoke." Odenzod stepped forward to meet his unexpected visitors.

Shaka remained kneeling so that she might look upon this strange man at his level. "We came upon Zelfore as we journeyed west," she said. "He spoke with us in a kindly manner and told us of this place. Who is this Zelfore that you hold in such high regard?"

"I do not rightly know, except that he twice appeared when least expected, and twice I owe him a debt of gratitude. Once 'twas so long ago I thought it only a dream, 'til it happened again. That time I was but a boy with the heart of a man. I journeyed into the West Woods, and as I crossed a river, I became swept away, pulled under water, dragged over rocks. I remember falling with water all around and rocks below—and then I knew no more. I awoke to find myself on the shore beneath the waterfall, and I remembered a dream, or so it seemed:

"'There you are,' a voice bellowed, and someone grabbed me by the arm. He lifted me away from the water as if I were no more than a leaf, and I just looked at him with eyes of a thousand questions. 'I am Zelfore,' he said, and nothing more. And then I found myself awakening upon the shore, coughing water from my lungs.

"Many winters later I journeyed in search of new lands. I ventured far, beyond where people tell tales of their travels. But in unknown lands come unknown perils, and I found myself in a snowstorm with wind so fierce that I buried myself in the snow to wait for the storm to pass. I lay in the darkness wondering whether this bed would be my last, but then a hand pulled upon my arm. I arose, and though I could barely see the hand that held me, I knew it from my dream. I followed, and Zelfore led me to these caverns. I remember he said, 'You know not the role you play,' and then he was gone.

"I have lived in these caverns ever since, for years beyond my reckoning, and no man or woman has ever disturbed my peace. I have shelter and protection here, and fresh water seeps through the hills. In time I discovered passages that lead to deep chambers and a door to the west on the far side of the hills."

"An opening to the west—that would help our quest greatly," said Shaka.

"And what is your quest?" asked Odenzod as he leaned upon his axe and stroked his beard.

"We seek the clearing of the West Woods and the fulfillment of the prophecy," Shaka declared. "I am Shaka, the Guardian of Tarzetta Trail, the keeper of the arrows, and this is Laney, the Sorceress from the West. Help us now, for surely this is your role as spoken by Zelfore."

As Shaka spoke, Laney came forward, not a lost girl but a mysterious cloaked figure aglow in the dancing flame of Odenzod's torch.

"The Sorceress from the West!" Odenzod gasped. His eyes opened so wide they might have fallen onto the floor had not his head been turned upward to gaze in wonder at Laney. "If Zelfore sent you, then I am at your service."

"Then lead us to the West," Shaka said without hesitation. Laney nodded.

"I can do as you wish," said Odenzod, "but I counsel against that. The way is long, and we must arrive ere the dawn. After night departs in the outside world, you shall not be safe underground."

"I fear not the rising or the setting of the sun," said Shaka. "Pray tell what troubles you."

"When darkness flees from the sun, the caves come alive and suffer no man or woman to pass," said Odenzod.

"Yet you live here," Laney observed.

"The caves and I are as one," said Odenzod. "When the caves sleep, I am awake, and when the caves awaken, I go to sleep. But you cannot sleep as I do. We must reach the western side before the dawn."

"Then let us start right away," said Shaka.

"Very well," said Odenzod, "but the way to the west joins many passages, and some hold dangers that bravery alone cannot overcome. Courage serves none who lose their wits—beware! There is dark magic in these caves, and the brave have much to fear!"

He started forward, but then a thought came to him, and he turned to Laney. "Sorceress," he said, "pray touch my arm that I might feel the power of your charms. Such strength shall be needed ere we reach the western rim."

Laney did not wish to disappoint Odenzod, either by refusing to touch or by touching to no avail. She looked at Shaka, who simply nodded. Laney turned to Odenzod and laid her hand upon his oak-like arm. Odenzod closed his eyes, took a deep breath, and then exhaled slowly. "Now I am ready!" he proclaimed, opening his eyes and giving Laney a nod of appreciation. He stepped toward the west, and the others followed.

The open chamber that seemed so vast with its dripping water echoing from wall to wall quickly narrowed into a passage not much wider than Odenzod. He was able to walk standing erect, but Shaka and Laney had to bend over and take care not to hit their heads. The passage wound this way and that, but ever in a westward direction, and always downward. The farther Laney went, the heavier her heart became, as if the hills above exerted an unseen force upon her. The still air grew more stuffy with each step.

The passage forked, and then forked again, but Odenzod knew the way and never hesitated. His torch flickered as air blew from one of the side passages, but he was careful to protect the flame.

They came to another passage, this one with the stale odor of mold that had grown for countless generations. As Shaka passed the opening, her stomach retched. She leaned against the cave wall vomiting, coughing, until finally she caught her breath.

"'Tis mold," said Odenzod. "Not all foes have swords or fangs."

"'Tis not the mold—'tis this," said Shaka as she held out her hand so that the light of the torch shone upon her wound.

"Gargartar spiders!" exclaimed Odenzod. "When did this happen?"

"But a moment before you came upon us," said Shaka.

"Then you haven't much time. We must treat the wound at the eternal pool. But that is far out of our way." He paused for a moment and then said, "Come quick! We have no choice."

Odenzod led them at great speed through a series of passages. Shaka struggled to keep up, and stumbled more than once as fever laid hold.

"Almost there," said Odenzod, and sure enough moments later their passage opened into a cavern of such size that all the walls and ceiling disappeared into the darkness. And when they entered the cavern, not ten paces in, Odenzod stopped before a pool of water, smooth as glass.

"Lay your hand in the water," said Odenzod. "Many crystals of old came from the hills above, and powerful crystals remain. Every drop of water in this pool has passed through those crystals, and there is a healing power that is as potent as any. The water is pure and cool. Let us all drink of it."

Laney filled her canteen and Shaka's, and they both drank their fill, marveling at the crisp, clean taste.

"It's like water, but it's not—I mean it is, but it's more," said Laney, not sure how any drink could be so refreshing.

"Your friend must sleep to break the fever," said Odenzod, "but there is no time. We must go. You must arrive at the western door before the break of day."

Shaka's breathing eased, and she looked about as if awakening from a dream.

"You're getting better," said Laney hopefully.

"That shall not last," said Odenzod. "We must make haste. The farther we go, the less your friend shall be able to travel."

Sure enough, Shaka's strength began to wane, but her will never wavered. Onward she went with dogged persistence even though soon she knew not where she was or why. Her mind entered a fog, and she could maintain but a single thought—don't stop! When Laney called out to her, she did not answer. When the dogs barked, she did not heed.

For what seemed like an endless night, they wound their way through the maze of caves. But then Odenzod stopped and turned to Laney.

"Do you hear that?" he said.

Hisses and gurgling noises came from up ahead. Tak and Gallia growled, ready for whatever Shaka might command, but Shaka stood in a daze.

"They dare not challenge the Sorceress from the West," Odenzod said. "Stay close!"

Laney found Shaka's hand and together they crowded toward Odenzod's torch. The sound grew louder as they approached and came to a side passage—and there, they knew, was where the creatures lay.

Odenzod thrust the flame of his torch toward the center of the opening as they approached. The hissing became so loud that Laney fancied she would feel it on her face, and as she dared look into the opening, countless sets of glowing eyes stared back at her.

Odenzod hurried past, and the others followed on his heels. Soon the hissing all but disappeared. They could feel fresh air up ahead, and they raced toward it. But as they passed a vent in the cave, the torch flame danced . . . and died.

"I need no flame," said Odenzod. "The way is near straight from here. We must hurry!"

Shaka knew not where she was or even who she was, but somewhere in her mind she knew to follow the hand that guided her. Tak and Gallia stayed close to her.

Finally the cave began to open, the walls retreating, the ceiling rising such that even in the total darkness Laney could sense the change.

"Almost there," Odenzod puffed, now a ways ahead of the others. But no sooner had he said those words than, with a thud and a gasp, he found himself flat on his back on the ground.

Laney, with Shaka in tow, caught up to Odenzod, but she could see nothing in the impenetrable darkness.

"The way is blocked." said Odenzod. "If the door to the west isn't opened before sunrise, it shall not open for another day. When the cave awakes and finds you here, boulders shall tumble and crash. You must reach the door!"

Laney squeezed Shaka's hand, hoping for a reaction. "Shaka," she pleaded, but she got no answer.

In the darkness, Tak nudged Laney, letting her know that she must take the lead. Everyone was counting on her.

Laney swallowed her fear as she stepped past Odenzod and explored the boulders with her hands. "They're huge," she said, "but maybe I can get through." She dropped her pack and crawled into a gap at the wall of the cave. The hole went through to the other side, and Laney moved quickly, fearful that the rocks might shift. As she poked her head and shoulders out the other side, stones fell all around her, like hail at the edge of a storm. She clawed at the wall and floor of the cave, and a moment later she was through.

Tak and Gallia barked encouragement. Laney raced ahead as fast as she dared, using her walking stick to feel the ground ahead.

Odenzod moved Shaka back from the boulders, as one might guide a sleepwalker away from danger. Tak and Gallia kept close to Shaka's side.

Then Odenzod laid down his axe and with his bare hands began pulling boulders away from the pile. Such was his strength that he moved them as if they were made of packed snow instead of rock. The largest ones he couldn't budge, but soon he had made a pass large enough for himself, Shaka, and the dogs.

He took Shaka's hand, and she followed. It seemed that with each passing moment she fell deeper into a trance.

"Hurry!" said Odenzod, as much to the dogs as to Shaka. They all ran toward the door.

Up ahead Laney slowed as the passage became more narrow. Her walking stick clanged against both sides as she swung it back and forth ahead of her. And then suddenly she hit the end of the cave.

Laney felt for a door handle, but all she found were bumps and ridges. She pushed against the rock, but it didn't budge. She felt for the outline of a door, but there was none. Then her fingers felt a small square hole. A keyhole, she hoped. Laney dropped to her hands and knees and searched for a key, but all she found were scattered stones and rocks and . . . bones!

She felt again the small hole in the wall. She stuck her finger in, and the hole went deeper than that. She stuck the end of her walking stick into the hole . . . it fit perfectly.

A door opened so suddenly that Laney nearly toppled through the opening. There before her stood a gaping hole, knee-high above the floor of the cave.

A blast of fresh air greeted Laney, delighting her spirits like never before. She could have stood there blissfully, but she needed to help her friends. She took one last deep breath of the sweet predawn breeze, and pulled her stick from the keyhole. She propped the door open as best she could with rocks, and then headed back into the cave.

Halfway back, she met the others. "The door's open," she announced.

"The weight of a mountain," said Odenzod. "Only a sorceress could open that door!" He bowed in respect as he handed Laney her pack.

But just then the ground began to tremble. "The cave awakes!" yelled Odenzod, and the first hint of daylight appeared ahead in the opening of the doorway.

Laney took Shaka's hand and pulled her toward the door.

"Fly!" cried Odenzod. "The dawn shall not wait!" But in spite of his urgency, he remained standing.

The tremble turned into a great rumble, and slabs of falling rock chased toward them. Odenzod dropped his axe and raised his arms.

Behind Odenzod, rays of first daylight shone through a vent in the cave. Laney looked back to see Odenzod standing, his hands reaching as high as his arms would allows.

"Fly!" he yelled as boulders tumbled about him.

The dogs raced ahead exerting what will they could to draw Laney and Shaka after them. As Laney ran, she looked back again, and amidst the dust and debris it appeared that the cave had fallen onto Odenzod's outstretched arms.

"Odenzod!" she yelled.

"Fear not for me!" he bellowed in reply, and the grayness of the light, his cloak, and the dust and debris made him appear to be made of the very rock that surrounded him. Indeed, he seemed to have turned into a pillar in the center of the cave.

Laney and Shaka tumbled through the west doorway and found themselves sliding down a hillside. When they came to a rest at the bottom, the ground shook from the torment of the cave, and the door to the west slammed shut.

At the bottom of the hill, Shaka lay so still that Laney feared the worst. But then she saw the steady rise and fall of Shaka's chest. Laney carefully wrapped an extra cloak around Shaka and let her lie where she had fallen. Then Laney, Tak, and Gallia stood watch as Shaka slept a dreamless sleep.

As the sun climbed past the early morning hours, Shaka stirred. Gallia nudged her, and Shaka opened her eyes. She sat up and looked around.

"What happened to my hand?" she asked, looking at the pair of red holes atop a mound of swollen flesh.

"You don't remember? A spider, I think. It was dark."

"We found a cave, and now we are here—where is the cave?"

"We went through to the west," said Laney.

"The night has passed me by," said Shaka.

"You don't remember Odenzod?" asked Laney.

"That sounds like a name not easily forgotten," mused Shaka, shaking her head.

"The door—" said Laney. "We need to see if it will open. We left a friend behind."

They climbed back up the hill, but where a door had appeared before, all they could see was rocky hillside.

"I don't understand. It was here. We came out right here," said Laney.

Shaka waited patiently while Laney continued to search in vain. When Laney finally gave up, she leaned heavily on her walking stick, and simply shook her head.

"Come sit," said Shaka, "and tell me your story."

After many interruptions from Shaka, Laney finally finished telling all that had happened during the night.

"A dwarf?" said Shaka.

"I didn't say that."

"Could have been a dwarf," Shaka persisted.

Laney shook her head. "I remember he said, 'The caves and I are as one,' and then it looked like he turned into part of the cave."

"Then we can hope that he is safe," said Shaka. "We can do nothing more. But now you must rest, and from what you say, you have earned that and more. I shall keep watch, and when you awake, we shall continue our journey."

Shifting Paths

When Laney opened her eyes, she felt rested and strong. Shaka stood nearby twirling her walking stick.

Laney approached and imitated the twirling of the stick. "How's your hand?"

"'Tis stiff but getting better. Show me what you remember." Shaka poked at Laney's stick, batting it one way and then another.

But in Laney's hands, her stick felt lighter than the time before, and no longer awkward. She whipped it with a swoosh of air, and though Shaka easily parried the blow, the sound of the impact left no doubt that Laney wielded her stick with confidence and force.

"Good—let me see more!" Shaka pressed Laney even harder.

Tak and Gallia watched with keen interest hoping that somehow they too would be included in the game.

Shaka and Laney exchanged attacks and parries, and although Laney could not penetrate Shaka's defenses, she showed no signs of giving up.

"You have much strength today," said Shaka. "We shall save the rest of it for our journey."

They readied their packs, and soon they were off. They encountered a snowstorm around midday, but the dense trees sheltered them from most of the snow and wind, and within an hour the storm had passed. Then, as fortune would have it, they picked up a path that weaved westward around steep hills, zigzagging past centuries-old trees. As it curved around one of the larger trees, the path forked.

Shaka stopped and leaned on her staff. "Neither path is true west," she said. "They may join again later, but I think not. You have been in these woods before. You shall choose."

"What? How?" Laney stammered.

"Let your staff point the way," Shaka instructed. "You have knowledge and powers that are hidden but perhaps not lost. Hold the staff before you, and command it to choose!"

Laney held her stick with both arms extended and willed it to move, but the stick remained as still as if it were planted in the ground.

"Patience," said Shaka.

"I feel ridiculous." Laney closed her eyes and held her breath, but nothing changed. She let out her breath and threw down the stick in frustration.

But her disappointment was interrupted by laughter. "Well done!" Shaka proclaimed through her chuckles. And Laney could see that the stick had come to rest pointing directly toward the path on the left.

"That's crazy!" said Laney. "You think I did that?"

"No," Shaka laughed. "But someday you will. For now, I am content that the fates have chosen."

They started down the left-hand path, Shaka still chuckling to herself. After just a few steps, Laney looked to the right to see whether the other path tracked close to theirs, but the other path was gone. Out of the corner of her eye, she glimpsed something moving, and she instinctively turned her head in that direction. "The trail . . ." she started to say, but stopped.

"The trails shift—I told you that," Shaka explained. "Do you not remember?"

"I remember you saying that, but I never thought I'd see it."

"Did you truly see the path shift? Are you certain of where it lay? Maybe 'twas always as you see it now. 'Tis easier to believe that memory plays tricks than that age-old paths pick themselves up and move about. But I believe the latter. You may judge for yourself."

"So, if we follow the path backward, we'll end up someplace else?" Laney pondered. "Or perhaps we'll end up where we started but not remember that place?"

"I choose to always look forward," said Shaka. "If I take a path into the West Woods going forward, I leave the path when I wish to return."

"So much seems strange to me," said Laney. "I need to find out who I am and where I belong, for both of us."

"The Sun Stone and the coming of the syzygy shall give you your answers at the clearing, or before," said Shaka. "Do not give up hope."

Laney had hope, and she could push aside many of her fears in the light of day. But the day was drawing to an end, and the setting sun let darkness seep into her thoughts. She worried what the night might bring. Wolves hunt at night.

The Bridge

Before the last glow of twilight departed, Shaka found a small clearing where she built a fire. Although there were no natural barriers to offer protection, she and the dogs would know if anything dared to approach.

Laney quickly fell asleep while Shaka and the dogs kept watch. Shaka sat with her crossbow cocked, resting in her lap, her eyes peering into the darkness.

Gallia smelled the first wolf. She let out a low growl, and Shaka knew what that meant. "Steady, girl," she said in a hushed voice.

Shaka gazed into the darkness, turning in every direction. She fancied she caught a glimpse of eyes, but they disappeared as she raised her crossbow. Quick as a cat she turned to look behind her, and again she saw a pair of eyes vanish in the trees.

"I can take them," said Shaka to the dogs. She could tell the pack was small, and she welcomed the challenge.

But the wolves kept their distance, and all the while their numbers grew. By halfway through the night, the pack had doubled in size, and then doubled again.

Then somewhere in the distance came the sound of snarls and yelps—someone or something else was out there! The noise grew louder, and the wolves that had threatened Shaka fled to join the fray. Not until the approach of dawn did the noise cease, and only then did Shaka dare to close her eyes.

As the sun cleared the horizon, Laney awoke, but a dream lingered—a woman with a green violin. Laney sat up, half expecting to hear the music.

Tak and Gallia lifted their heads, and a moment later Shaka awoke as well, tired yet restless. "We must hurry," she said. "'Tis late, and there is a mystery we must explore."

They readied themselves quickly for the day's journey, and Shaka led them toward the ruckus from the night before.

Soon Shaka could smell the unmistakable odor of wolves, yet her instincts told her the danger had passed. And then they came upon the first carcass.

A great wolf lay nearly cut in two through its shoulders and back. Several paces away, more wolves lay dead, scattered with heads and limbs cleaved clear off their bodies.

Laney couldn't believe this had happened such a short distance from where they had slept. Dozens of wolves lay dead.

Shaka studied the ground. "A great warrior did this deed," she said. "Only one set of boots has trod these grounds." She pointed to one of the wolves with a huge gash in its side. "'Tis not a cut from a knife or sword," she continued. "'Tis the wound of a battle axe."

"Odenzod!" Laney exclaimed. "He's alive!"

"I know not, yet our warrior has feet of a giant and the stride of a child. I would expect as much from the one you describe as Odenzod." Shaka followed the bootprints with her eyes and nodded. "He came from the east and returns to the east, where we left the cave. I choose to believe that you are correct. But now we must continue our journey to the west. I think you need not fear for the welfare of Odenzod."

With Tak by her side, Laney followed Shaka, matching her stride. They came to a steep incline, and Laney cast a glance regretfully to either side.

"We cannot go any other way," Shaka said, reading Laney's thoughts. "We will be out of the valley soon enough, and then we shall see."

Laney grabbed hold of whatever her hands could clutch as she climbed past saplings and shrubs. Shaka led skillfully, and soon the slope crested.

Laney stayed close behind Shaka, and after a time asked to hear more about the West Woods. With the sun still at their backs and long hours ahead, Shaka began her tale:

"The stories of old tell of the changing day, when a wind from the west carried black smoke and mist along the forest floor, and with it a smell of rot and death. The wolves howled that night like never before, and folks who lived in the woods felt a chill in their bones as if the cold hand of death lay upon them. Many without shelter perished that night and the nights that followed as wolves attacked without mercy. Thus began the battle with the wolves that goes on to this day. The wolves seem to disappear and reappear at will, and tracking them is perilous. Familiar paths seem to shift, and those hunters who venture far from home are few and fortunate to return."

"But you hunt them," Laney mused.

"Yes . . . and my reasons are close to the heart—as close as my brother. Gardron was his name. When I was but a girl, my father taught us how to live off the land. He also taught us the dangers of the Woods. But my brother, ever headstrong and bold, feared no danger. Eager was he to become a man.

"We lived beyond the edge of a village in a cottage built by my father. Indeed, we lived among the trees of the new growth, the fingers of the West Woods. My father at times dared to venture deep into the Woods, 'where boots have seldom trod,' he would say, and always my brother begged to go with him. 'Shaka can chop wood,' Gardron would say. 'Then who shall mend the fence?' my father would reply.

"But the lure of the Woods proved strong for Gardron, and one day he ventured into the forest, following our father's trail. Gardron's tracking skills could not match my father's stealth, and soon Gardron became lost. After a time, he managed to find his way home, a testament to my father's teaching. But as my brother had our home in his sights, wolves had him in theirs. He saw them not, 'til they fell upon him, tearing his flesh from his bones. Two girls heard his screams, and one foolishly ran to help. Had she been a powerful warrior, still she could not have saved my brother. A wolf leaped upon her, and she fell with teeth tearing into the arm she raised to protect herself.

"Two arrows pierced that wolf as it fell upon the girl. Then more arrows flew through the trees and two more wolves lay dead. My father burst through the brush in a rage, letting out a yell no one had ever heard from him before or since, but he was too late for my brother.

"My father carried Gardron's body and the injured girl back to the house and lay them both on his bed. He held my brother and wept while my mother restrained her grief and tended to the girl. The girl kept saying, "Help Gardron . . . help Gardron," until she fainted from her wounds. It all seemed like a dream, people acting in ways I had never known—my father weeping, my mother in command, my brother . . . no more."

Shaka paused as she wrestled with the memory, as fresh with the retelling as if it had happened the day before. "A wound of the body may heal with naught but a scar, but a wound of the spirit is a wound forever. My father changed—saddened and enraged beyond cure. My brother was gone, and along with him my false belief that he mattered not to me. Now I see him only in my dreams.

"My father basked in his rage to hide his sorrow—he hunted the wolves with a vengeance. He made a necklace with their ears . . . and another and another. The wolves learned to stay away. But my father was not content. He followed their retreat deeper and deeper into the West Woods. And then one day he did not return. Perchance he lost his way on shifting paths, or wolves came upon him in numbers too great for any man . . . but I think not. He was too good a huntsman and knew the land better than any who are at home among the trees. No, I think there must have been something else, something evil beyond what we know. . . . Villagers searched for a fortnight, but they never found him, nor any sign he may have left behind.

"When I had grown enough to wield it, I took up one of my father's crossbows, and the wolves learned to respect me. They became like ghosts of the forest. But recently attacks outside the villages have begun anew, and I know the wolves are breeding and gathering in great numbers in the heart of the West Woods. I know that the time has come to challenge them before they challenge us."

Shaka stopped for a moment and looked off into the distance—but whether lost in thought about days long past or weighing her options for the day ahead, Laney could not tell.

"So why don't the people put together an army and march upon the wolves, or burn back the trees?" Laney asked as they started walking again.

"For many of us, our way of life is the woods. We would never set fire to them," said Shaka. "And marching upon the wolves . . . that is not as easy as it sounds. The forest is vast, maybe endless beyond the Northwest Mountains, and the wolves will not meet an army in open battle. Some men and women have tried such an attack, but the wolves are too cunning. As well as some of us know the Woods, the wolves know it better. No, such attempts have not met with success. More often than not, no wolves are slain, and not all who set out return. The wolves have developed a taste for human flesh, and too often they know how to get it."

"But you hunt them."

"Yes, if any dare approach my home or show themselves when I travel the land, I hunt them. For if they do not fear me, they will hunt me. With every season, they become more bold. The syzygy is coming only just in time."

As the day wore on, their course gradually straightened, and presently Laney realized they were following a trail. "Where did this path come from?" she asked.

"The paths come and go," Shaka replied. "To find one underfoot is a blessing, but they cannot be trusted. We must follow this one only so long as it heads due west, and we must be wary. A path can ascend to a cliff or dip into the wetlands or wander to nowhere. But I can read the land as well as any, and I shall not allow the paths to lead us astray."

"What's beyond the Woods?" Laney asked.

"To the east—villages, of course. They stretch farther than I have traveled. And beyond the villages . . . who is to say? There are many lands I have not seen."

"But you go where you want, and you do what you want—no one tells you what to do."

"We each answer to our conscience. Is that not enough?"

"But you're the Guardian of Tarzetta Trail—what does that mean?"

"That post lay abandoned, and I knew it waited for me. I volunteered when no others would, and the elders agreed that I should guard the Trail. I have served for many years. My charge is to watch and protect the homes that border the West Woods. The strong must help the weak. I let the wolves know that they cannot roam within the reach of Tarzetta Trail."

"What else is beyond the Woods?" asked Laney.

"To the north, a journey of many moons, lies the great ocean. Tales tell of a frozen wasteland far beyond that meets the sea, but I do not know. The ocean goes on beyond the knowledge of anyone I have ever met. South, there are more villages, and then beyond Aborra, lesser woods and lakes of water so pure you can see fish at the very bottom. Farther south the land becomes hot, and farther still the sun scorches the earth such that nothing will grow. I once traveled to the edge of this land and heard stories of people and their animals inhabiting such places. But when I looked for myself, I saw nothing as far as any eye can see on a clear day. I think talk of folks living in these lands is not true, and that nothing exists but the sand, the wind, and the sun. I dared not venture far beyond its borders."

"What about the other side of the Woods, to the west?"

"Mountains, and beyond that no one knows," said Shaka, "but I suspect nothing good. The black fog came from the west, and any land that could spawn such evil must itself be cursed."

The sun climbed high in the sky as the travelers made their way along the path. The trail began to slope upward, gradually at first but then at times so steep that Laney would put a hand on the ground in front, fearful of accidentally leaning back and tumbling down the hill. Her breath came heavy, and her pack seemed to gain weight with each step. But just when she thought she could go no farther, Shaka held up a hand in warning. Tak and Gallia sniffed the air. Laney froze, listening for a clue.

"The trees give way," said Shaka. "We must be cautious." Sure enough, several paces ahead the trees opened to a rocky ravine. "Follow closely!" Shaka commanded as she led the way to the rim of a cliff.

Laney tried not to look down, but she couldn't help glancing over the edge. She focused on Shaka's feet, trying to match her step for step so as not to fall behind. Tak stayed close to Laney.

They continued along the edge of the ravine until they met a trail cutting its way downward into the rocky face of the cliff. "Our way has been forced to the north," Shaka said. "We cannot correct for that unless we get past this ravine. There is no telling whether this trail is clear to the bottom, but we must take the chance."

They made their way carefully along the narrow descent. Laney kept one hand on the rock face, leaning into it, making sure she stayed as far from the edge as possible. She counted each of her steps, pretending the magic number needed to reach the bottom was just a few more.

Presently the trail widened, and Laney felt more at ease. "Have you done this before—cliffs like this?" she asked Shaka.

"I have traveled far, and sometimes I use the paths," said Shaka. "Hills and cliffs do not stop me."

"Who made these trails?"

"They have always been here, for as long as anyone can remember," Shaka replied. "Hunters and trappers used them long ago. But when the forest changed, sometimes those who ventured along the paths never returned. Those who did claimed that the paths shifted from day to day, or that new paths would appear, or old paths would disappear."

"So nobody uses them anymore?"

"Few dare to challenge the paths," Shaka explained. "Even with a lifetime of tracking and hunting, I must be ever cautious when I set foot upon them. My father in his day had a sense for them like no one else. He could not command the paths, but more often than not he knew where they would lead and when he could trust them."

"You miss your father."

"Every day of every season—and my mother, and my brother."

Laney wondered whether she had a family, and whether they were looking for her. How long had she been away from them? Did it all start when she lost her memory, or long before?

As Laney's mind wandered, so too did her steps. And when she placed her foot too close to an undercut edge, the earth gave way.

Her arms flailed wildly, hands clutching at air. Her walking stick clattered onto the path . . . and she fell.

Quick as a snake, Shaka lunged for Laney's ankle. "Haaaa!" she yelled, grabbing tight with both hands.

Laney's back and head slammed into the side of the ravine. Dazed, Laney turned her head every which way, finally realizing she hung upside down. She flung her arms skyward toward Shaka, but her pack weighed her down. Again she tried, and again she fell short.

The cliff's edge began to crumble. One last time Laney whipped her arms skyward . . . and her hand found Shaka's wrist.

The edge gave way beneath Shaka's chest, but Tak and Gallia bit into Shaka's clothes and tugged with all their might. The dogs held fast, and Shaka pulled Laney to safety. Soon all sat breathless against the wall of the cliff.

"I should have led with greater care," said Shaka.

Laney shook her head. "You saved me, and you're apologizing? I need more friends like you." She put her arm around Tak. "And you too."

They rested for what seemed like only a moment to Laney, but the sun moved noticeably toward the west. "We must go on," said Shaka, and she helped Laney to her feet. "Stay close, and I shall guide us ever so carefully."

They continued along the trail as it cut into the ravine, but instead of leading to the valley below, it took an unexpected turn and once again rose. Shaka decided the best choice was to follow it and see where it might lead. But each bend in the path revealed yet another upward slope, with no end in sight. Then finally a change—not the descent they were hoping for, but a bridge. One hundred paces at least it spanned to the other side of the ravine. The bridge lay flat and sturdy as though it were steel and concrete, but whatever its structure underneath, its top resembled the earthen path beneath their feet, though snow and ice lay more heavily upon it. The bridge had no handrails, nor even a curb to protect from an accidental misstep.

Shaka marveled at the bridge. "Such a bridge would be easy to defend," she said. "Those who made this bridge were wise in the ways of battle. Two might walk abreast yet no more."

"I think I've learned something about myself," said Laney. "I don't like heights."

"No other way leads to the west, but you need not fear. This bridge is every bit as wide as the trail. It matters not what lies outside the path, if you do not stray."

The bridge had no handrails, nor even a curb to protect from an accidental misstep.

Laney looked to the far side of the bridge. If she ran, she could be across in less than a minute. "I can handle it," she said.

"Good. We shall send Tak and Gallia first. Then you shall go, and I shall follow."

Tak and Gallia seemed to know the discussion was about them, and they stepped to the foot of the bridge. "Go now," said Shaka.

Tak moved carefully, and Gallia followed. About halfway across, Tak stopped and barked. But then a moment later the dogs continued to make their way across. Soon they stood upon the far side.

Shaka put her hand on Laney's shoulder. "Careful," she said. "This bridge has stood for ages beyond reckoning, but not all who set foot upon the likes of this reach the other side."

Without a word Laney stepped onto the bridge. It felt no different from the forest floor—at first. But as the sky surrounded her, a chill raced down her spine. Her legs stiffened all the way to her toes. She willed her feet to move, a step, another step—and then the wind came. Her hair whipped her face, and she swayed like a sapling in a storm. Her pack pulled this way and that, as if it would wrestle her to the ground far, far below. She dropped to her knees.

From across the bridge Gallia barked encouragement—or something else. Laney crawled, reaching wide with her fingers to steady herself against the gusts that came without warning. The bruising of her knees spurred her on ever faster.

And then suddenly she stopped. Before her lay a gaping hole.

As she looked, the crumbled far edge appeared unimaginably thin, such that she might touch the bottom with her fingers while gripping the top with her thumb.

Whether a trick of the wind or the fancy of her mind, Laney felt as if the hole were drawing her closer, and she started toward it. The wind whistled across the gap, sucking away bits of ice and snow. She dropped to her belly and pulled herself forward, gripping the outer part of the bridge with one hand and the lip of the hole with the other. A chunk came loose in her hand and fell to unknown depths, and as she looked after it, she felt her head spin. The wind howled in her ear as if it carried spirits of wolves and echoes of long-lost souls calling for another to join them. She put her chin onto the ground so that she wouldn't see the emptiness beneath the bridge. She pulled herself forward.

"Almost there!" Shaka yelled from behind, but a gust of wind carried away her words.

Then Laney's knee loosed a chunk of ice clinging to the outer edge—down it fell to such depths that Laney never heard it strike the rocks below. But now she reached the end of the hole. She hurried back to the center of the bridge, rising off her belly to her hands and knees. She looked up to see the other side, not far away. Tak stood there with his eyes locked on Laney, as if his stare would keep her safe. A final gust of wind pushed with all its might, but Laney held on, and as the gust faded, Laney reached the end.

Shaka followed a moment later. "Your fear is now behind you," she said to Laney. "I made light of this bridge, but crossing it took much courage."

Laney felt foolish, having crawled like a child. But had she looked back during the crossing, she would have seen Shaka on all fours as well.

"Fear summons the brave," Shaka said as she lifted Laney's chin. "Real courage is acting in the face of fear, and you have done that."

"I just follow your lead," said Laney as she looked into Shaka's eyes.

I can't imagine what I'd do without you, Laney thought . . . *and I don't want to find out.*

Malleos Thorns

The path ended at the far side of the bridge, but Shaka led Laney and the dogs at a fast clip nonetheless, bypassing thickets and rocky slopes. And just when Laney started thinking their progress couldn't get any better, they happened upon a path from the south, curving westward.

"Good fortune is with us today," said Shaka as she stepped upon the trail and gazed into the distance where the path twisted and turned out of sight.

The trail proved a welcome relief, as it wound its way uninterrupted by streams or fallen trees. At times it threatened to carry them off course, but always it seemed to make a correction just in time as Shaka assessed whether to abandon it. Presently the path took them toward a break in the trees and joined the edge of a cliff.

"Good fortune is with us?" asked Laney, not happy to see another cliff. "Maybe if I had wings instead of feet!"

Though the path remained wide, the travelers proceeded in single file, keeping away from the edge. Laney followed close to Shaka, matching her stride, concentrating on each step.

After what seemed like hours to Laney, the path and the valley began to converge. The once-sheer cliff now had an obvious slope that began to flatten. Laney felt a sense of relief as she looked ahead—but they weren't there yet.

Without warning the path gave way. Rocks and stones tumbled all about. Dogs yelped. Laney covered her head. Shaka clutched her crossbow.

Down they went, to the bottom of the ravine.

Brambles and brush helped break the fall. Shaka landed feet-first in a patch of thorns, as walking sticks and arrows clattered past her. Laney came to rest facedown with a thud that took her wind and made her head spin. They both got to their feet and looked to the other to make sure they were okay. Shaka stepped away from the thorns, carefully pulling them loose from her cloak. "Were you scratched by the thorns?" she asked, and the tone of her voice conveyed much concern.

"No, but your hand is bleeding," Laney replied.

Shaka held up her hand, and sure enough droplets of blood spread along a cut from her thumb to her wrist. Laney could tell by the look on Shaka's face that this scratch was something more than it appeared.

"Malleos thorns," Shaka lamented, "anything but malleos thorns! I must think fast—there is no time."

"What?" said Laney.

"The malleos thorns have a poison that makes the mind see and hear what is not there." Shaka paced back and forth, shaking her hand with each step. "Already I feel a fire in my hand, and my eyes see colors in the white of the snow," she said. "You must not be near me when I fall completely under the spell. You must go—now! Tak and Gallia will go with you. They are not safe with me either, and you will need them. I shall track you when the spell passes."

"But where will we go?" asked Laney.

"West—Tak and Gallia shall guide you. You must go—now!" Shaka insisted. "It has begun, the spell—I can feel it." Shaka unbuckled her hunting knife. "Take this," she said, and fastened the belt and blade around Laney, who stood at a loss for words.

Then Shaka looked at Tak and Gallia. "Go with Laney—go quickly!"

If Laney was unable to see the change already taking effect on Shaka, Tak and Gallia certainly sensed it. They barked urgently, commanding Laney to come with them. Tak pushed her with his head and then grabbed her cloak in his teeth and pulled.

Shaka, now shivering, sat down and crossed her legs. "Hurry," she said, "before it is too late. You dare not stay. Soon I will no longer know myself nor anyone else, and the land my mind travels shall be treacherous. There is no telling who or what I might harm."

Laney reached for Tak, and put her arm on his mighty shoulder. They looked at each other, and understood. Tak turned his gaze one last time toward Shaka, and then both dogs barked farewell.

Laney felt neither hope nor purpose in moving forward, but she would go wherever Tak and Gallia might lead. Gallia bounded in front, while Tak kept by Laney's side, and together they headed westward.

The hours rolled by. Laney had no idea where they were going or what she would find when they got there, but she put her faith in Tak and Gallia. Eventually they struck a path, and although it seemed to head substantially north of where they should have been going, they followed it anyway. As Laney looked to either side, she could see that hiking off the trail would be challenging. The land rose on one side, and brush spread along the forest floor on the other.

When their shadows began to foretell the coming of dusk, Laney said, "Tak, where are we going to stop?"

Tak looked up at her and barked in reply, and Laney sensed that he understood.

Soon they came to a fork in the trail, and the split was marked by a towering tree with protruding roots the size of tree trunks. Tak and Gallia sniffed the air along each path. Laney began to circle the tree, marveling at its size and majesty. On the far side she came upon a deep hollow between two large roots. "Tak!" she called, and both dogs came running.

"Let's sleep here," she said as she climbed onto the roots and swung her legs into the hollow. She slid into the opening and found her footing.

Tak and Gallia waited for Laney to get situated. She had enough room to lie down and clutch her pack as if it were an oversized pillow. The hollow was larger and darker than she expected—and warmer. It extended well below the frost line, and for Laney it felt almost like being indoors. She stretched and yawned . . . and that's when she felt the first snake.

A rattlesnake den! She jerked her hand away—too late. Fangs pierced her wrist—searing pain. She screamed . . . leaped . . . flung her arms, hurling a snake into the air.

Tak and Gallia growled and snarled, guarding her retreat—across the path, into the trees. Laney stumbled, caught herself, then stopped with a gasp and a wail.

Head spinning, she sat, her back to a tree. She pulled up her sleeve—two blood-red holes. Her heart pounded. Sweat rolled down her forehead.

"Tak, what have I done?" she moaned.

Tak lay down beside her, sharing the warmth of his fur. Gallia did the same.

A fog descended upon Laney's mind. She looked up to the tops of the trees fading into a gray sky, darker it seemed each time she blinked. She rested her wounded arm in her lap.

How did it all go so wrong? she thought, just before her world went dark.

The Great Arch

Laney opened her eyes to bright sunshine with Tak and Gallia still lying by her side. Gallia barked and Tak nudged Laney affectionately. The fog had lifted from Laney's brain, and she felt almost normal. She looked at her wrist, and she was pleasantly surprised to see no swelling—just two punctures. Little or no venom had entered Laney's wrist—either that or she had made a miraculous recovery.

Laney had no appetite, but she forced herself to eat and drink, and she shared her rations with Tak and Gallia.

"Shaka would have had us on our way an hour ago," she said after her last bite. She got to her feet and hoisted her pack onto her back. "We'd better get started."

Tak took the lead. Whether by instinct or some other power of nature, he knew where they must go. He headed onto the left-hand fork of the path to make up for the northward drift in their hike the day before. But soon the path curved this way and that until eventually they were once again headed northwest. They reached the crest of a small hill, and Tak turned off to the left, leaving the trail behind. Without a word, Laney followed.

The day wore on, sapping Laney's strength. She leaned heavily on her walking stick, and her pace slowed. The forest grew more dense, with roots crisscrossing the ground, and overhead the canopy seemed restless as wind whistled through the top branches, freeing clumps of snow, sending it showering onto the travelers. They stopped twice for a brief rest, but Laney felt no stronger afterward. Tak barked encouragement, and Laney did her best to keep up.

As the daylight began to fade, Laney saw something large in the distance, so large that the trees could not obscure it from view. Tak started to lead Laney away from it, but Laney felt an urge to see what it might be. Tak barked twice, but Laney walked toward it anyway.

Tak and Gallia reluctantly followed, and soon all could see clearly a great structure, an arch made of stone. Though less tall than the trees, the arch stood resolute against the dual assaults of time and weather, its majesty defying the elements. The carvings upon its surface survived in vivid detail in spite of pitting and stains from birds, leaves, and even the black fog. Though Laney could not understand all the symbols and imagery, she recognized that carved into the individual stones were stories from a time long gone. Images of people and animals, scenes of work and play, and carvings of nature and the heavens, all conveying a sense of harmony, order, and reverence. Laney knew without a doubt that she and Tak and Gallia had found the great arch of Peltston and Buroakville. She felt excited, almost exuberant, like the weight of her journey had been lifted from her—pain and worry, gone. But Tak again barked twice.

"I want a closer look," said Laney.

But Tak snarled and growled, and Gallia joined in the protest.

A tangle of vines encircled the arch, but they clung close to the ground and offered no resistance—at first. Laney trampled upon them as easily as if they were nothing more than leaves. But then her foot sank into a hole hidden by the undergrowth—a hole so deep that it swallowed half her leg. She put her hand into the vines to keep from falling. She leaned and pulled. Her leg wouldn't budge. And just as she wondered how that could be, a vine tightened around her wrist.

Behind her Tak barked—not a warning but a call to action, as if he knew that Laney needed nothing more. And Laney understood. She unsheathed the knife that Shaka had given her and thrust the point into the thickest of the serpentine tangles. The blade sank into it as if striking warm butter. Black ooze flowed from the wound. The vine recoiled. Another grabbed hold—and another, trapping

Laney knew without a doubt that she and Tak and Gallia had found the great arch . . .

both legs—pushing, pulling. Laney struggled to keep her balance. She slashed—left, right. Injured tangles sprang back. She freed her wrist. Then her legs. Finally the vines lay limp.

But instead of retreating, Laney stepped up to the great arch.

Now Tak and Gallia barked and growled an urgent warning, both of them sensing a threat from the ancient structure before them. But Laney felt an inexplicable urge to step through the arch. The barks faded in her mind, and a moment later her hand touched the surface of the majestic stone. She removed her glove to feel it with her hand, oblivious to the cold. And then she looked up. The structure seemed even more immense now that she stood almost directly under it. She ran her hand along the front face of the carved stone until she approached the inside of the arch. Then she allowed her hand to pass into the shadows.

As soon as her hand touched the first inside stone, she felt a welcome warmth, as if she were standing before a campfire. And without another thought, she stepped beneath the arch.

Tak and Gallia charged forth together, determined to be by Laney's side regardless of the danger. But in just one step, Laney had disappeared from view. A moment later, both dogs leaped through the arch.

As Laney disappeared beneath the arch, so too did the world around her, and in that instant she marveled at how that could be—darkness, floating, utter silence. Then, like a flag when the last breeze passes by, her mind fluttered one final time—*it's not real*—and she lost all conscious thought.

An Unsolved Mystery

Life returned to Laney with a whoosh and a swirl, and when she opened her eyes she had the distinct feeling that she had somehow been transported far away. Flat on her back, she could tell by the trees that she remained in the forest, but beyond that she wondered where she might be, and how. She tried to sit up, but her head spun, and she felt weak.

"Lie still a moment longer," came a familiar voice.

"Shaka!" said Laney, not quite believing her ears. "You're here!"

"Yes, Laney, I am here." Shaka moved into Laney's view. "And now so are you—though I thought for a while I might lose you."

"Then you're okay—how did you find me? Where's Tak, Gallia?"

"They are here," Shaka reassured her. "Lie still a moment longer. Your strength will return quickly now."

Laney tried to sit up, but instead all she could do was roll onto her side. "I feel dizzy—what happened?"

"Rest now," said Shaka.

"How did you find me?" Laney persisted.

"Can you not see that we are now where we were yesterday—the bottom of the ravine, with the malleos thorns?"

Laney managed to sit up and look around, and sure enough they were exactly where they had parted ways.

"How did I get back here?" Laney asked.

"You never left," Shaka replied. "You have been under the spell of the malleos thorns. Fortunately I know how to treat such wounds, but the effects are powerful. You have recovered faster than I had hoped, but then I have always said that there is more to you than you can imagine."

"But you—your hand—you were scratched. And I see blood in your hair," said Laney. She could see dried blood had dripped from Shaka's scalp down the side of her face.

"I have my share of scrapes," said Shaka, "but not from the thorns. I took a blow to the head when our trail gave way. When I came to my senses, I found you here, under the spell of the thorns."

"That's not what happened," Laney protested. "I left with Tak and Gallia, and we went without you for two days. We found the arch to Buroakville and Peltston. I passed through the arch, and now we are here. I remember it."

"You may remember it, but that does not mean it happened. The malleos thorns cast a powerful spell."

"My arm—I was bitten by a snake." She pulled up her coat sleeve and saw that her wrist was bandaged.

"Your arm was punctured by a pair of malleos thorns," Shaka explained. "I cleaned and dressed the wound."

"No, it was a snake!"

Shaka made no reply.

"The arch has carvings on each of its stones—stories I think," said Laney. "Do you know that? It is massive, almost as high as the trees, with heads at the top, watching."

"Yes," said Shaka, "That is true, and how you would know this I cannot say. 'Tis possible the Sun Stone you wear has given you powers of sight beyond what I can explain."

"And you said that the arch might make someone appear at another time or place," Laney added.

"For a sorceress, yes, I did say that," Shaka admitted. "But you have been journeying in a land of dreams, for I have tended to you ever since your fall. 'Tis possible you know the arch because you once came through it, and the malleos thorns have stirred that lost memory."

"Tak can take us to the arch," Laney offered, unwilling to believe that her experience had not happened exactly as she remembered.

Shaka looked at the scratch on her own hand. Then she looked up at the sky, and shook her head. "We have lost much time. We must resume our quest and be content to live with this mystery. I shall choose to believe that you had this journey in some manner that I do not understand."

Shaka helped Laney up, and helped her with her pack.

Tak and Gallia barked, eager to move on. They weren't used to being caught unawares by crumbling paths and poisonous thorns.

"We must hurry," Shaka said, and there was no mistaking the urgency in her voice.

Wolves

The trees grew larger as the travelers advanced toward the heart of the West Woods, the oldest growth in the forest. The underbrush, struggling in the shadow of the immense canopy, easily gave way to the travelers. They rested only twice before the sun began to sink toward the horizon.

As evening approached, the wind from the west brought change to the air. A breeze reminiscent of spring blew through Laney's hair, and she raised her head to welcome the relative warmth. But Shaka looked worried. "A westering sun leaves a chill in its wake," she said. "Something is amiss."

Suddenly Tak and Gallia barked. Shaka stopped and sniffed the air. "'Tis coming," she said, and although her voice remained calm, Laney could tell that something was terribly wrong. "Come," said Shaka, "we must move to higher ground—quickly!"

They headed up a gentle slope, and Laney matched Shaka stride for stride as they quickened to a trot. Then Laney smelled something foul—a rotten odor that so repulsed her nostrils, she instinctively opened her mouth to breathe. But the odor could not be avoided, and as it entered her lungs it polluted her spirits, sending a death-like chill down her spine. And then a dark, patchy fog rolled and swirled past her hastening feet, tumbling its way ahead of her. The fog moved with the speed of the wind, and Laney, Shaka, and the dogs were soon surrounded. The fog turned darker as it grew thicker, climbing from their ankles to their knees.

They struggled as the hill became steeper, but the land worked in their favor. The fog slowly retreated until it became nothing more than hazy wisps swirling at their feet. Soon it faded altogether. But the stench remained, and looking back, they could see the fog continue to climb. Laney's legs felt as heavy as tree trunks, but still she charged up the hill.

Just as she felt she had reached her limit, the trees opened up before them. The dogs, leading the way, suddenly stopped. They had come to another ravine.

They could follow the edge wherever it might go, but looking both left and right, they could see a gentle descent. The dark fog again began to drift across their feet.

"We must climb the trees," said Shaka. "The wolves shall soon be coming."

The wolves! Laney shivered. "What about Tak and Gallia?"

"We cannot carry them," said Shaka, "but we must protect them from the wolves."

Shaka peered over the cliff, a vertical drop with the nearest shelf a distance no dog or wolf could survive. "Give me your pack," Shaka instructed as she removed her own. She retrieved rope from her pack and cut two lengths.

Working quickly, she secured a pack to each dog with the pack's straps and the rope. "We shall lower the dogs onto the shelf. They will be safe from the wolves until daybreak when we can retrieve them. We must hurry." Shaka spoke softly to Gallia, hugged her, and led her to the edge of the cliff. Gallia whimpered, but she understood. They heard a wolf howl in the distance behind them and

another wolf answer. Black fog now rose quickly past their knees, its clammy rot seeping through their clothes and onto their skin, sending shivers through their bodies. Shaka wrapped part of Gallia's rope around a nearby tree and then several times around her arm, and she called to Gallia to go over the cliff. Against all instincts, Gallia obeyed. Shaka quickly lowered Gallia until the rope was no longer taut. Then she knotted the rope to the tree. She repeated the process with Tak, but Tak resisted going over the edge. The wolf howls came closer, but Tak had no fear—he wanted to fight. "Go!" Shaka commanded, but still Tak stood fast. He looked at Laney, his charge to protect, but when their eyes met, Laney echoed Shaka's command—"Go," she said, and Tak turned and stepped over the edge.

By the time Shaka fastened the second line, the wolves were almost upon them and fog floated up to her chest. The stench nearly overpowered Laney, her head spinning, her stomach retching. Shaka grabbed Laney's arm and pulled her to a towering tree. "Now, climb like never before!" she yelled, and as she spoke those words, the first wolf charged. Black, it seemed, with the swirling fog.

An arrow flew and then another, as Shaka cocked, aimed, and fired with incredible speed. Two wolves fell dead, and then two more, but others came from behind, more wolves than Shaka had arrows in her quiver. Shaka leaped into the tree. The wolves leaped after her, their jaws snapping at her feet, but Shaka was too quick. In no time she had caught up with Laney, safely out of reach—or so they thought. The black fog kept rising.

When Shaka looked down, she could no longer see the wolves. Some remained at the foot of the tree, but others came to the edge of the cliff—they smelled the dogs. The beasts howled in frustration, and several plunged into the ravine as they jostled and pushed, so excited were they at the prospect of fresh dog. Shaka and Laney could hear the yelps as wolves tumbled toward the rocks below.

Laney and Shaka climbed as high as the thinning branches would allow. Then they held fast to the trunk and to each other. But the black fog continued to rise.

Xinni and Ogmo

The sound of the wolves below grew to a fury. The black fog crept up, almost to Laney's feet. Shaka looked up at the thinning branches, trying to judge whether they should dare to climb higher. She pulled hard on the branch just above her head. It broke loose.

But the black fog came no higher—it was no match for the wind blowing through the tops of the trees. For now, Laney and Shaka were safe.

The first light of dawn crept over the horizon. Laney could now see her breath. The temperature had dropped precipitously in the hours before dawn, and in spite of the remarkable warmth of her cloak, she felt chilled to the bone. She and Shaka climbed back down the tree, and when they reached the bottom, they could see that white frost covered everything in sight. All remnants of the black fog had disappeared. Even the foul smell was gone, as if it had all been a bad dream. But not far from their tree, the dead bodies of four wolves lay motionless, stiff in the icy breeze. Shaka retrieved her arrows, the golden arrows of Protection, from their marks and cleaned them in patches of snow. Then she called to her dogs: "Tak, Gallia—ready to come up?" Both dogs responded with enthusiastic barks.

Laney had worried what the black fog might do to the dogs, but by all appearances they seemed to have suffered no ill effects. Their tails wagged, and Tak and Gallia displayed their typical boundless energy.

"Are we ready?" Shaka asked as she untied the packs from the dogs and handed Laney hers. Laney made no answer, knowing full well that Shaka's question wasn't really a question. But Laney didn't mind. She was ready to get as far away from there as possible.

Shaka led them away from the ravine and back on track to their final destination. She seemed anxious about their progress, and pushed onward without a morning break. By the time they stopped for a rest, the travelers had covered half a day's journey.

While Laney rested her legs, Shaka stood twirling her walking stick, then jabbing and thrusting with it. She seemed lost in another world, focused on invisible foes, striking here and there, and then just as quickly fending off blows from multiple directions.

"Who taught you that?" asked Laney.

Shaka planted her stick in the semi-frozen ground. "My mother," she replied. "My father taught me the crossbow, and my mother taught me to use sticks. She was a practical woman, able to use anything at hand for whatever she needed. A stick became a weapon, or a hanging rod, or a pole to reach beyond her grasp. A sock would warm her foot, carry nuts from the forest, and protect her hand from the heat of the frying pan. She could do a thousand things with a length of rope."

"What happened to her?" asked Laney.

"After my father failed to return from the West Woods, my mother fell into a deep sorrow. Never again did I see joy in her face. She performed her duties as a mother, teaching me the ways of the woods, but her heart no longer belonged at our home. I grew up, and we grew apart. The day came when she left with no warning, only a quick goodbye. She headed into the woods a fortnight before a syzygy."

"What! To fulfill the prophecy?" asked Laney.

"I think not," said Shaka. "She knew the significance of the syzygy, but she also knew that the other signs of the prophecy were absent. No, I think she chose that time because somehow the time chose her."

"You said this is your third magical syzygy. What happened with the first two?"

"The first time I was ill with fever, and the syzygy came and went before I recovered. Yet I knew that was not the one. I wore the Sun Stone then, and it gave me an understanding beyond the vision of others. The second magical syzygy proved to be much like the first—the forest, the wildlife, the spirit of the Woods all remained calm. But this third one is different. The forest is uneasy, the wolves are restless and gathering, and the earth has trembled more than once. This third syzygy is the one. I now wear the azure crystal of second sight, but even without it I would know. I see the signs all around me, even in my dreams. And you are here."

Gallia saw the first squirrel. Or perhaps she heard it or smelled it. Tak was too busy keeping an eye on Laney, and Shaka's attention was focused on the path and where it might lead. The squirrel, halfway up the trunk of an imposing oak, made an almost imperceptible chattering sound and then darted to the other side of the tree. Gallia barked, and immediately Shaka froze, listening and sniffing the air.

"Squirrels," she said. "Where there are squirrels, there is food."

"You eat squirrels?" Laney asked.

"Not squirrels—nuts. Where there are squirrels, there are nuts stored for the winter. Look about you—there are more squirrels than trees." Sure enough, as Laney looked about the trees, she saw first one squirrel, and then another and another. And soon, whether because she now knew where to look or because more and more squirrels came to gawk at the travelers, Laney saw more squirrels than she could count.

"There must be hundreds of them," she said in wonderment. "How did I not notice?"

"They have only just arrived," said Shaka.

The squirrels began darting from tree to tree, and with each passing moment, they became more numerous. Soon they all seemed to be heading in the same direction as Shaka and Laney, scampering on either side of the path. As some vanished into the distance, more came upon them from behind. Shaka and Laney continued down the path, until suddenly it disappeared. Shaka approached the end of the path, and then a smile spread across her face. There before them stood a camouflaged cottage, so like the trees that they had almost run into the front door.

"The path plays a trick, but maybe not a bad one. We shall see. Let us be bold!" And with that, Shaka strode to the front door and reached for the knocker.

But before she could touch the door, it opened. A thin, young woman with long blue hair stood before her.

"Welcome!" said the woman. "We do not get many visitors—just the squirrels." She smiled pleasantly. The padding of heavy footsteps approached from behind her, and a moment later a gaunt figure of a man peered around the door. He towered over the woman, his head nearly the same height as the doorway. A swan tattoo on both sides of his face accentuated hollow cheeks and a high forehead.

"We saw no signs of life all day in our travels, until suddenly these squirrels," Shaka said. "Are you their keepers?"

"Oh no—they look after themselves," the woman replied, "but they do store nuts from many trees in and about our home—enough for them and us. No, if anything, they are our keepers. I am Xinni, and my husband is Ogmo—he seldom speaks, but when he does, those who are wise, listen."

Ogmo nodded and smiled.

"I am Shaka, and with me are Laney, Tak, and Gallia. Our surprise at finding an open door this deep in the West Woods is surpassed only by our gratitude. We are pleased beyond words."

"And we are pleased to have visitors," Xinni replied. "Come inside. We have soup and drink, and of course plenty of nuts. You shall tell us of your travels. The dogs are welcome as well, so long as they respect the squirrels."

The travelers stepped into the cottage, and right away Laney could see that there were even more squirrels inside than out—squirrels carrying nuts, eating, and running here and there. Huge piles of acorns and other nuts occupied every corner and covered much of the floor such that Laney had to be careful where she stepped.

"The day grows short," Xinni said. "You shall stay the night. We have but one room for you to share—still, a small room is better than an open sky. Tonight you shall be warm."

"Many thanks," said Shaka. "Such hospitality is most welcome in the wild."

"Come lay down your packs and sit," said Xinni. "I have food prepared, plenty for all, and we shall talk over supper."

"Welcome!" said the woman. "We do not get many visitors . . ."

Xinni led them to a table near the center fireplace, and they shed their packs and winter wear. Laney rubbed her hands together and felt the warmth return. She and Shaka took a seat at the table, while Tak and Gallia sat beside them on the floor. Gallia twitched now and then, suppressing the urge to chase a squirrel.

Xinni stirred a cauldron hanging above the fire and then fetched bowls for her guests. "Ogmo will pour some of his special brew—it soothes the spirit," said Xinni.

Soon everyone had a bowl of stew and a cup of pale liquid.

"Ogmo's drink is like honeysuckles in spring," said Xinni. "Every time I taste it, winter disappears from my thoughts and sunshine enters my mind. There is nothing like it when snow blankets the forest and wind pushes at the door. The making of the brew is one of Ogmo's secrets that many would like to know."

"In all my travels 'tis the finest ever to pass my lips," said Shaka, who alternately tasted and sniffed the pleasant liquid.

Laney wondered if she had ever tasted anything like it.

Ogmo smiled, though still he had not uttered a single word. He fetched more candles for the table and then sat with his guests.

The squirrels continued their activities seemingly oblivious to everyone at the table, and to the dogs as well. Laney couldn't help but watch them.

"That one is Astril," Xinni said, pointing to the gray squirrel closest to Laney. "And Shale, and Hazella." She pointed to others. "Squirrels are clever—they have more sense than most people you meet. They all have a sense for the woods—know where they are and when to seek shelter. Astril gives me the best nuts, and I take him with me at times when I venture outside. He likes to sit on my shoulder." She winked at the squirrel.

Shaka raised her cup. "To unexpected friends, and the virtues of squirrels."

Xinni raised her cup. "To safe travels."

They drank and ate heartily. Xinni told them story after story about the squirrels, often bringing laughter to her lips.

Presently Shaka noticed a lute resting against the wall.

"Do you play?" asked Xinni.

"Music is in my blood," Shaka responded.

"Then you must honor us with a song!" Xinni retrieved the lute and handed it to Shaka.

Shaka plucked each string, savoring the sounds. "'Tis an honor to play such a fine instrument," she said, and began playing a song handed down from her mother:

She is the sun; he is the moon,
Dancing afar to an eternal tune.
He is the moon; she is the sun,
He smiles because she's the only one.

The sun and the moon, the moon and the sun,
The sun and the moon, having their fun.

Gone for a night, the moon reappears,
Smiling now from ear to ear.

He'll catch if he can, his dearest sun,
He'll never give up, he'll never be done.
The sun and the moon, the moon and the sun,
The sun and the moon, having their fun.
Now one to my left, one to my right,
The brightest they'll be on any a night.
He rises, she falls, soon out of sight.
Waves crash ashore with all their might.
The sun and the moon, the moon and the sun,
The sun and the moon, having their fun.
The next day he's late—she's already gone.
He searches the sky 'til just before dawn.
He's falling behind—he can't turn to see
That she chases him boldly across land and sea.
The sun and the moon, the moon and the sun,
The sun and the moon, having their fun.
Day turns to night. Night turns to day.
Years upon years all slip away.
The dance still goes on the very same way.
It shall evermore, every night, every day.
The sun and the moon, the moon and the sun,
The sun and the moon, having their fun.

Shaka's voice trailed off as she plucked the song's final note. Then she looked up. "Thank you." She nodded to Xinni and Ogmo. "For a moment I forgot my journey—such is the magic of music."

"Such sweet sounds," said Xinni. "We must have more drink and another song!"

But Shaka declined. She knew they had much to discuss, and she and Laney needed their rest. The candles had burned low, and empty bowls and a spent jug marked the hour as late.

"Then tell me of your journey," said Xinni. "Though there is much that I can guess with the syzygy just days away, I expect there is more that you can tell. You are drawn to the heart of the West Woods—that much is clear."

"Yes," said Shaka, "our destiny lies there. Laney came from the west but has no memory of her journey, or even herself. She seeks to remember. I heed the message of my dreams and a calling that I have felt all my life. I must challenge the evil in the Woods—the wolves and whatever drives them. I must put an end to the black fog. Laney, I know, has a role to play. She does not believe so, but I have no doubt."

"I have lived my life in these woods and understand much," said Xinni. "I feel the spirit of the trees, I smell the purpose of the wind, and I taste the flavor of the rain. I see the essence of every person, a glow that clings like a shadow, and yours, Shaka, shines so very bright. Laney, yours is different. It is like a rainbow in the summer mist. I do not know what it means, except that something about you is most uncommon."

"Thank you," said Laney, trying to be polite, "but I don't know my past, and don't know what to believe."

Ogmo nodded but remained silent.

"You need to believe in the unbelievable, and it will be true," Xinni explained. "Your strengths are a mystery, but they are more than you imagine."

Laney didn't know what to say, but she held Xinni's gaze. Xinni smiled, and in spite of neither saying a word, there was no awkward silence.

Then Shaka asked, "How came you and Ogmo to live so deep in the West Woods?"

"We have been here for more seasons than I can recall," Xinni replied. "We came in search of the origin of Ogmo's crystal, one of great power. Some crystals have a way of calling their bearer to the source of their power, the one place where the effects of the crystal never fade. Such was the way with Ogmo's. It gives him vision beyond what any can see, and enables him to command the forces of nature that surround our home. Here even the black fog is no match for Ogmo. But now that we are here, we dare not leave because without this crystal at full strength, we cannot stand against the black fog and the wolves. We shall remain here until such time as the prophecy is fulfilled or until we no longer draw breath."

"Are there others like you, trapped in the West Woods?" Laney asked.

"None so close that we know who they might be," said Xinni. "Perhaps we are the only ones . . . but I think not."

Then Xinni turned again to Shaka and said, "The time has come to atone for the sins of our ancestors."

"What's that mean?" asked Laney.

"If the stories we tell children are indeed true, then the black fog and all that it brought to the West Woods came to us through our own greed and folly," Xinni explained. "The Northwest Mountains, the keepers of the clouds, are the sacred guardians of the West Woods. Water from their slopes feeds the streams and rivers that give life to the forest. One day whispers began to spread of great treasures beneath the mountains—gold and gems of unspeakable value. Whence these stories came, I cannot say, but a tale oft repeated is one believed to be true. And so the time came when men dared to set out for the sacred mountains. They came with tools to climb and dig, and they journeyed to the tallest peaks, for surely the greatest mountain would bestow the largest jewels.

"When they reached the mountains, men labored through two moons chiseling, gouging, defiling the sacred slopes in their lust for treasure. Traders and hunters came and went, bringing food and whatever else treasure seekers might desire. Word of crystals and veins of ore spread throughout the land, the tales growing taller with each telling.

"What happened next is truly not known. No one survived, and no one has dared venture near that mountain again. But the last of the traders and hunters to visit before all was lost claim that the digging opened a hole to a cave. The cavern boasted such size that all who sought treasure could enter and explore. Such a cave must have been sealed since before the time that man or beast roamed the land, and such a cave should not have been disturbed.

"That night, without warning, a plume of rot rose from the cave and settled upon the Woods, and as quick as stench can move through air, madness swept through the forest. Wolves possessed with a fury came down from the mountains and out from hiding to claim the Woods, and no one could withstand their savagery. In a single night the very essence of the Woods changed as completely as if day had perished and only darkness remained.

"There is an evil presence now—that cannot be denied. Some say that it hides within the black fog, while others say that it *is* the black fog, waiting to take shape in some beastly form. Regardless, the darkness grows. If it is not defeated soon, it shall become so emboldened as to reign supreme, and the West Woods shall fall beyond redemption in our lifetime and perhaps many more.

"Not even the wisest of the wise can say for sure whether or how the West Woods may be restored. Perhaps you know in your hearts what others do not. Perhaps the final chapter of this tale is yours to tell."

So ended Xinni's story, and silence followed. Then Laney asked a question that had been nagging at her since the start of their journey. "What's going to happen when we get to the clearing?"

Xinni looked at Ogmo, but he sat motionless and spoke not a word. So Xinni responded, "No one can say what you shall find in the clearing, but those who know the prophecy believe that this is the time and place where the West Woods might be freed. I know not how that may happen, but I believe in your quest, and I believe in you. You must believe in yourself."

"I'm not sure I know how to do that," said Laney. "I know so little about myself."

"You know that others believe in you," Xinni replied. "Is that not enough?"

"I don't know. Maybe it has to be."

"The hour is late," Xinni said after a moment. "Tomorrow you must start as the sun greets the day—the syzygy is drawing near. But now you must sleep, and may the blessings of this evening afford you pleasant dreams."

Xinni led her guests to a small room, and although there were no beds, thick furs on the floor provided both padding and warmth. Shaka and Laney thanked their host, and Tak and Gallia wagged their tails.

As she stood in the doorway, Xinni said, "Before you leave, Ogmo will speak."

. . . a field nymph in a headdress of meadow reeds and wildflowers.

The River

The bow danced on the strings of the green violin, harder and faster into the Vivaldi solo. And while at first the image of the violin filled Laney's mind, it began to shrink until it was little more than a grasshopper in the hands of a most unusual woman—a field nymph in a headdress of meadow reeds and wildflowers. The woman gazed into the distance, and then looked straight at Laney and winked.

Laney stirred in her sleep, and the woman and violin vanished, and instead Laney heard a child's laughter. "Do you like it?" the child asked. A crayon drawing of Laney appeared, the same one she had seen at Shaka's cabin.

Laney sat up with a start, catching the image in her mind before it could disappear to wherever it is that all dreams go. Whose voice was that? She searched her mind but still could not penetrate the surface of her vast sea of memories. The darkness of the room was complete, and she lay down again, knowing that she would need whatever remaining sleep she might get.

Laney awoke late and did her best to hurry, not wanting to miss breakfast. She knew that when Shaka decided to resume the journey, there would be no delaying their departure. But to her disappointment, there was no breakfast—not that their hosts hadn't offered, but Shaka felt an urgency that could not be swayed by any promise of food. By the time Laney left the bedroom, Shaka already had her pack on and was pacing the floor, carrying Laney's pack. And before Laney could say, "Yes please, I would like some breakfast," Shaka was hoisting Laney's pack into position and fastening it about Laney's waist.

Xinni saw the disappointment in Laney's eyes and said, "I put some of the finest nuts in each of your bags—something to remember us by in the days ahead. May your travels bring you all the answers that you seek." She stepped forward and hugged Laney, and Laney hugged her back, not wanting to let go. In just one short day she had developed a fondness for Xinni and this home in the woods, and even the squirrels.

"Thank you for your kindness," said Shaka. "I hope that someday we shall meet again."

Xinni put her hands on Laney's shoulders and looked her square in the eyes. "Heed your dreams and visions," she said. "They will become more vivid the farther you travel. One day they will be real." She paused to allow her words to sink in. "Knowing who you are is not as important as believing what you can do."

Astril, or a squirrel of similar appearance, chattered, seemingly in agreement.

Ogmo smiled and turned to Laney. "A squirrel will change your life," he said directly to her. "It has already happened."

Laney looked curiously at Ogmo and then back to Xinni for an explanation.

"There you have it," said Xinni. "Ogmo's wisdom. When you understand it, seize the moment!" Xinni turned and bowed to Ogmo. Laney and Shaka exchanged confused looks.

Xinni turned again to Shaka and Laney. "Ogmo commands the paths in these parts," she said. "He will make sure that your day's journey brings you to safety. Do not stray from the path, and you shall encounter no foe during the light of this day. After that, you must trust to your skills and whatever powers you can command. Heed the days—they are few indeed before the syzygy. You must not be late!"

They headed toward the door, and said their final farewells. "From this day forward, I shall think of you and Ogmo every time I see a squirrel," said Shaka. "Know that your kindness will always be remembered."

And Laney said to Xinni, "I don't remember who I am, but you made me feel like a friend—thank you."

Xinni smiled. "I am glad."

And with that, the travelers started down the dirt path. Both Laney and Shaka turned to wave, and Laney looked over her shoulder more than once. Her heart sank as Xinni and Ogmo's home quickly faded into the forest.

They traveled onward, uneventfully, until they came upon a river that interrupted their path with rapids and mini waterfalls turned to ice. In places the ice had been amassed by the river's spray and then carved by the wind into spectacular natural sculptures, some with holes in the center and icicles hanging like candles dripping to dry. They marveled at the beauty of the scenery.

The path continued on the far side of the river, but getting there would not be easy. Shaka shaded her eyes and looked in both directions.

Crows flew overhead. Some perched in the nearby trees, as if curious about what the travelers might do.

Shaka set her pack down and took a few careful steps onto the ice. Then she retreated back to the riverbank. "Parts are frozen hard, but the water beneath runs fast."

"Xinni told us to stay on the path," said Laney.

"Yes, but there is no path across these waters. We must choose our own crossing, and for that I need a better look."

Shaka led them a short ways off the path to an evergreen as tall as any they had seen all day.

"Wait here," she said as she removed her crossbow and quiver and set them beside her pack. She leaped to the lowest branch and climbed as easily as if she were ascending a spiral staircase. Tak and Gallia stood at the base of the tree keeping watch.

Laney sat down, welcoming an opportunity for rest. Shaka's crossbow and quiver lay within reach, and Laney couldn't help taking a closer look. She ran her hand along the stock and then onto the string, or wire as it seemed—hard and immovable as steel, it felt to Laney. She picked up the crossbow, expecting it to feel as heavy as a rock, but to her surprise it weighed no more than a pair of boots. She looked down the stock as if she were aiming to shoot. Then she put down the crossbow and reached for one of the arrows in Shaka's quiver. It felt light as straw, yet hard as stone. Black feathers graced the end, and a thin weave of golden thread encircled the shaft. Laney removed her glove to feel the feathers, at once both soft and stiff. Then she ran her hand along the golden thread and down to the tip. She barely touched the point, yet it effortlessly sank into her skin, and she jerked her hand away, dropping the arrow. Without thinking, she stuck her finger into her mouth and sucked away the drop of blood, as if that would suck away the pain, a sting greater than she would have expected. And then suddenly a feeling of déjà vu swept over her—nothing she could place, but too pronounced to ignore. She shook her head, as if that might clear whatever blocked her memory, but instead the déjà vu passed, replaced by a wave of nausea.

All this time, Shaka climbed higher and higher until the branches became too thin to go any farther. She reached out and pushed aside the greenery, and it parted like a window curtain. Dazzling sunlight greeted her, and she squinted as she gazed upon the course of the river. But with its twists and turns, the river soon disappeared from view, and Shaka realized that she would need to explore on foot.

She hurried back down the tree and dropped from the lowest branch. "There is no clear way forward," she said, "but we must go."

Tak and Gallia wagged their tails as if setting out for their first walk of the day. Laney started to get up, and then stumbled.

"Do not touch the arrows," Shaka warned. She could see that her crossbow and quiver were not exactly where she had placed them.

"Are they poison? Why didn't you tell me?"

"'Tis not poison," Shaka replied, "but there is more to it than just a sharp tip —a power bestowed upon their creation generations ago. But you do not believe in such things, do you? Before our journey's end you may discover much that you do not believe."

The vertigo and nausea passed quickly, leaving just a hint of embarrassment in their wake. Laney followed Shaka the short distance to the bank of the river, where Shaka once again surveyed the ripples and ridges in the ice. She stood silent for a moment, and then spoke as much to herself as to Laney. "The river flows south. Better to head north, to higher ground."

The river twisted and turned, disappearing into the forest—they would not know what lay ahead until they arrived. With each bend in the river, Shaka assessed the potential for crossing, and each time she decided to go on.

Soon, however, they heard the distant roar of cascading water. The sound grew until finally they rounded a bend, and there in the distance stood a waterfall of such height and majesty that not even winter's coldest breath could put it to rest. And leading up to where the falls plunged, boulders channeled the water into a series of rapids.

Shaka pounded her stick in frustration. "In neither tales nor songs have I heard of any such falls." She shook her head. "We must turn back."

Tak barked, and Laney reached to pet him.

"We may rest but a moment, and then we must look to the south," said Shaka, "but I fear there is no safe crossing."

Laney took off her gloves to retrieve a snack, the nuts that Xinni had given her.

As Laney and Shaka sat near the river bank, more crows gathered in the trees above, cawing loudly.

"They don't seem to like us," Laney observed.

"The crows are never friendly," said Shaka, "but I do not think they will follow us once we are clear of the river—and that must be soon."

The squawking grew louder, as if the crows were taunting the travelers. Then with a flutter of feathers, one of the birds swooped down and snatched Laney's glove. She swung a hand at the crow, but it was gone in an instant, flying through the trees.

Lightning fast, Shaka unslung her crossbow and fitted an arrow. "Destiny!" she yelled, aiming with the azure arrow. But the bird was almost out of sight. Dozens of trees stood between her and the crow. She let the arrow fly, an impossible shot, and it disappeared into the woods. In the distance a crow cawed, and others took flight away from the travelers.

"Follow me," said Shaka.

"No way," said Laney to herself.

"My aim is true," said Shaka as she picked up her pack and led the way into the forest.

After a distance far greater than Laney imagined any arrow could travel, Shaka abruptly stopped and held up a hand. She sniffed the air, then walked ahead, still signaling for Laney and the dogs to stand still.

Shaka bent down and surveyed the ground, then picked up something—the glove! She then returned to where Laney and the dogs stood waiting.

"Someone is here," she declared, handing Laney the glove with a hole through both sides of its cuff. "My arrow is gone, and in its place I see signs of a heavy boot. We dare not follow, but we must be vigilant, even when we sleep. We know not whether we are being followed, but for sure we know that we are not alone."

Laney poked her finger through the hole, then pulled the yarn to cover it as best she could. She was glad to have both hands covered again, but by now they were the type of cold that she knew would last all day.

"We have wasted much time," said Shaka. "We must head back the way we came and either cross where we left the path or try heading south. I fear that neither is a good option."

They retraced their steps as quickly as they dared. Eventually they rounded the last bend before the trail, but although they had returned to the place where they had left the path, it was gone. All traces of it had disappeared from both sides of the river.

"Gallia, Tak, find our scent—find the path!" Shaka commanded, yet she knew it was hopeless. The dogs went off in different directions, but soon they returned, unsuccessful.

"Gone," said Shaka. "We must find our way without it. This day is cursed." She gazed across the river. "We must look to the south."

They headed downstream, but soon they ran into more difficulties. Small streams fed into the river, and water raced beneath the ice as the land sloped ever downward. But then they came to a place where the river widened and flattened like a sheet of glass. Shaka looked intently at the ice.

"This will have to do," she said. She opened her pack and retrieved a coil of rope. "We shall tie ourselves together, and we shall tie our packs as well and drag them across the ice."

"That works for me," said Laney.

"Give me your staff as well," said Shaka. "I shall not have you poking holes in the ice."

She worked quickly, cutting and tying knots with the skill of one who has a lifetime of experience in the wild. "I shall tie the dogs as well," she said. "They can lead the way."

Laney was surprised by the length of rope that uncoiled as Shaka tied them all together. "I never travel anywhere without rope," Shaka said. "You never know when you might need it. Most things I can find or make in the wild, but not good rope."

When Shaka finished with the ropes, Laney was disappointed to see that both packs and the walking sticks were tied to her instead of Shaka. "You must follow me," Shaka explained, "and so the packs and sticks must follow you."

The rope stretched ten paces or more between each of the travelers, with both dogs tied to Shaka.

"Tak, Gallia, go steady!" Shaka commanded.

The dogs ventured out onto the ice. Shaka followed, and then Laney, dragging behind her the packs and sticks.

"Step where I step!" Shaka commanded.

"No problem," said Laney. She didn't know whether she could swim, and she didn't want to find out.

Shaka moved as though she were tracking game in the forest, her footsteps sure and light. Laney followed, and when Shaka got down on all fours and began to crawl, so did Laney.

Midway across the river, the wind had blown the ice clear of snow. As Laney looked down at the smooth surface, something beneath the ice caught her eye—a fish! It looked up at her, opening and closing its mouth as if trying to tell her

She stared, momentarily mesmerized by the lone fish . . .

something: *Hello there*—or maybe *Hold on there!* She stared, momentarily mesmerized by the lone fish, as unexpected to her as she must have been to it. This river, though but a finger of the sea, contained the magic of primordial life, the origins of all that lived both below and above the now-frozen surface. Gazing into the depths of water and time reminded Laney of how small and insignificant her role must be in any grand scheme of the universe.

Laney's rope pulled taut. "Keep moving!" shouted Shaka, looking over her shoulder.

With a swish of its tail, the fish disappeared, and Laney again began crawling toward the opposite bank. She looked back down through the ice several times, but whether because of the glare or the cloudy ripples in the ice, she could see no more signs of life.

"Tak and Gallia—forward! Go!" Shaka called.

Now almost across the river, the dogs barked in anticipation. But Shaka could see air bubbles trapped beneath the frozen surface, and as she moved her hands forward, the bubbles retreated from the pressure.

With a crack and a splash, the ice gave way, and Shaka fell through. She gasped to fill her lungs with air before the bulk of her clothes and weaponry pulled her beneath the surface. Her arms thrashed, sending ice and spray flying into the air. Then with a wild look in her eye, her face plunged into the frigid depths.

Laney, Tak, and Gallia tugged on their ropes to keep Shaka from being pulled beneath the ice. But then, to everyone's surprise, Shaka stood up with water only up to her chest. With a snarl she plunged forward, breaking the ice before her with her arms as she made her way toward the shore. She tried to pull herself back on top of the ice, but it crumbled with each attempt. Then she suddenly dropped down to her neck and stopped dead in the water.

Laney scrambled to the side and then in front of Shaka, where she and the dogs pulled with all their might, but the ice was too slippery.

"Stop!" Shaka yelled. "My feet are trapped! You shall pull me under." Struggling to stand erect in the current, she tilted her head skyward to keep her face above the water.

The riverbank lay teasingly close, but neither Laney nor the dogs had any slack to reach it.

"Must cut the rope!" yelled Shaka, her freezing hands fumbling for her knife, then raising it high.

"No!" yelled Laney with such power in her voice that Shaka's hand froze as if Laney commanded the blade. And then Laney rose up, fire in her eyes, like a sorceress from the tales of old. She raised her arms above her head as if summoning strength from the heavens, and then slammed the heel of her boot into the unstable ice. Her foot blasted through the fragile surface. Ice all around gave way.

Water rushed to greet Laney, but her feet found the river bottom just knee deep. Then with all the strength that her will could command, she pulled Shaka free, through shattering ice, until they both reached the shore.

Tak and Gallia bounded up the steep bank, and Laney struggled to follow with Shaka.

"We gotta get into the woods—out of this wind!" Laney yelled above the din of the barking dogs as she half carried, half dragged Shaka forward.

Laney sat Shaka against the trunk of a tree and tugged frantically at Shaka's wet clothes. The cloak fell away as if on command, but the garments underneath clung as if they had melted into Shaka's skin. Laney tore off her own soaked gloves and willed her fingers to grip Shaka's clothes.

When Laney finally pulled the undergarment off Shaka's arm, Shaka groaned in pain. What looked like a jagged scar, torn open, wept bubbles of blood and yellow rot. "What's this?" Laney demanded, unable to hide her shock at the sight.

"An old wound," said Shaka.

"Then why hasn't it healed?" Laney pressed.

"A bite wound from a West Woods wolf never truly heals. And when a syzygy approaches, all powers grow, including those of darkness. My wound shall fester until the passing of the syzygy. This has happened before, but now I shall not let it stop me—not so long as I draw breath."

"You're the girl who tried to save your brother, aren't you?" said Laney.

"Yes—foolish, and I paid the price. This wound is from long ago."

"Should we wrap it?"

"No," said Shaka. "I must let the foulness drain as it will. 'Tis open now because I cut it open —yestereve, ere I slept."

All the while Laney pulled fresh clothing from Shaka's pack and dressed Shaka as best she could. She removed her own cloak and wrapped it around Shaka.

"We've got to get you warm." She hugged and rubbed Shaka, but knew that wouldn't be enough. "Tell me how to build a fire."

"'Tis difficult the first time," Shaka replied through chattering teeth.

"I watched you do it before—just tell me what to do."

"Get sticks, all sizes, and dry leaves. Tak, Gallia, come keep me warm!"

Laney used Shaka's knife to cut the ropes that tied them together, then said, "I'll be right back."

She rushed off to gather sticks and leaves, and returned minutes later with her arms full. "Okay, what do I do now?"

"Brush away the snow. Then we shall do this together, but you need to be my hands—my fingers are stiff with cold. Get my tinderbox out of my pack."

Laney found the box and followed Shaka's instructions to get the fire started. But each time she struck her flint toward the tinder, the sparks danced up and away. She huddled close over the tinder, and struck the stone as hard and as fast as she could. And suddenly she saw a flicker, then smoke. She sheltered and nursed the flame, feeding it as Shaka instructed, and it grew into a fire the wind could not daunt. Laney then left to fetch more sticks. Soon she had enough kindling to last throughout the fading day and night.

Laney felt comfortably warm . . .

Shaka, Laney, Tak, and Gallia all huddled together beside the fire.

"If ever you deemed yourself a burden, think that no more," said Shaka. "Today is who you are."

Today is who you are. Laney thought about that. Her actions now defined her, and what she did today and every day thereafter would shape who she would become.

With the fire now blazing, Laney fished through the packs for food. She found some of the dried fruits and meat that Shaka had packed, and also the nuts that Xinni had provided. They shared water from Laney's canteen, warmed by the fire.

Laney discovered another cloak at the bottom of her pack and wrapped it around both herself and Shaka. Laney felt comfortably warm, but Shaka shivered and murmured strange sounds. *I have to keep her warm,* thought Laney. *There's nothing more I can do.*

Sights and Sounds

Laney twitched in her sleep, struggling against dangers she could not escape —earthquakes and chasms, wolves and black fog. Finally these nightmares faded, and she dreamt of a vast sea with glistening fish jumping, breaking the otherwise mirrored surface of the water. *They must be close*, she thought. She reached with both hands, but the fish were far, far away.

The image faded, and Laney opened her eyes to dawn's first light. Shaka no longer shivered, but her rasping breath revealed her ongoing struggle. The dogs lay against Shaka, sharing their warmth.

The fire burned low. *Should get some more sticks,* Laney thought. She arose carefully so as not to disturb Shaka.

Laney intended to keep the campfire within sight, but when she turned to head back, it was nowhere to be found. Her heart pounded. She headed in the direction she believed was back, hoping with each tree she passed that the familiar blaze would appear—but it did not.

Then, amidst the gray shapes of the trees, Laney saw a most unexpected sight—a girl! The girl wore a dress so long it touched the ground, and so wide at the bottom that Laney thought, *She can't be wearing that here!* Laney expected the girl to turn and greet her, but the girl remained motionless, even when Laney said "Hi." So she moved to face the girl, and said "Hi" once more. But the girl had her chin held high and stared into the sky.

Then, to Laney's surprise, the girl's dress parted just below the waist, and a miniature version of the girl peered out at Laney—same wide dress, only smaller, and hers too was parted below the waist—where yet another even smaller version of the girl appeared. And then another miniature girl peeked from beneath that dress, then another, and another. Each girl stood pale and frozen, yet Laney fancied she heard the largest one speak, and then the second, and the third, and so on.

"Why this?" asked the one looking toward the sky, her voice raspy as if she had asked that question over and over until she had nearly lost the ability to speak.

"When?" asked the next one. And then each successive version of the girl uttered a word or two: "So long . . . still . . . waiting . . . help . . ." Or maybe that was "hope"? Each voice carried a higher, softer pitch until eventually the voices disappeared altogether and all that remained was the thought of a sound, one Laney imagined a hummingbird or butterfly might make if anyone could hear it.

Laney touched the hand of the largest girl. It felt cold, hard like stone. The wind gusted—the girl's dress fluttered across her legs. The smaller girls all disappeared, and Laney wondered if they had been anything more than her imagination. She took a step back, and as she did, the wind swirled, and leaves from the ground blew skyward. More and more leaves swirled around Laney until she could see nothing else.

Can't be happening! Laney thought.

She closed her eyes for a moment, and when she opened them, the leaves had vanished, and she found herself standing before the campfire, with Shaka, Tak, and Gallia all staring at her.

"What?"

"You asked, 'How?'" said Shaka.

"How . . . are you?" said Laney. The vision of girls within a girl now lay buried along with so many of Laney's memories and dreams.

Shaka shook her head and looked to the rising sun. "I am weary," she said. "The cold has been a battle I am ill prepared to face—my fever grows worse. And already another day is upon us."

Gallia barked at Shaka.

"Yes," said Shaka. She patted her on the shoulder. "You are right—we must go before the sun climbs any higher."

That afternoon they found no trails to aid their progress, but the woods and terrain treated them kindly, and miles fell away faster than the hours.

When they stopped for their first break of the day, Laney said, "I had the strangest dream last night. I was a prisoner. I couldn't move. Someone yelled, 'She's dangerous!' and I think they were talking about me. Then the ground started to shake, and everything felt like it was falling."

"During the night, did you feel the tremor in the earth?" Shaka asked. "It lasted no more than a few breaths as you lay asleep."

"I don't remember that—is that what caused my dream?"

Shaka shook her head. "The tremor did not cause your dream. Your dream caused the tremor."

Laney shook her head.

"Surely this is true," said Shaka. "The Sorceress from the West may sway the elements of nature—so say the tales. I believe you have such power, unwittingly and without control. For nine days now the earth has been restless, starting the day you came to my front door. 'Tis by chance? I think not. The first time struck like thunder from the earth, a rumbling and shaking fit for a tale. Then upon your arrival at my home, the snow that rests upon my hillside let loose to bury you. And as we journeyed, twice the trail crumbled beneath our feet—frozen dirt as hard as rock. Where you go, Laney, the earth is restless."

"If I'm causing all of this, I don't know how."

"You must believe in your powers, for how else shall you learn to control them?" The tone of Shaka's voice left no doubt that she had grave concerns. "If your powers do not serve you, they shall surely work against us."

They both fell silent. Laney wondered what she could possibly do to prove or disprove her abilities.

In the afternoon, the gray sky cast a somber mood upon the travelers. They crossed two streams where harsh wind blew uninterrupted by the trees. Their battle to stay warm seemed harder, as if the cold accumulated every hour, like new snow piling onto old.

Shaka led them to the north anytime the westward trek became difficult. Then, after a brief detour, they would resume their push to the west. The forest seemed endless to Laney. She had confidence in Shaka's ability to lead, but Shaka stumbled more than once. When Laney caught up, she could see Shaka shivering.

Mostly they traveled in silence. Laney's worries about Shaka grew as the day wore on, and she began to wonder how Shaka would be able to continue.

Laney paid no attention to the wind whistling through the trees, but then another sound caught her attention.

They crossed two streams where harsh wind blew uninterrupted by the trees.

"Shaka," Laney called out. "Do you hear that?" They both stopped and listened.

"I hear nothing but the wind and the sound of your breath," Shaka declared.

"Listen . . . in the wind . . . it's music."

"You hear something that I cannot," Shaka said.

The music became louder for Laney, as if drawing closer. She fancied she had heard the music before—not that she could predict the notes, but each one sounded as if any other note would be wrong. She knew she wanted to follow the music to where it came from, or where it might lead her, and without asking Shaka she trotted ahead, toward the sound.

Shaka readied her crossbow and followed.

"It comes and goes," said Laney as she stopped and listened.

"You have powers that neither you nor I understand," said Shaka.

"There it is," said Laney as she turned. She plunged ahead through the trees, pointing as she ran, as if her finger would latch onto the sound. But then she stopped and caught her breath. "The music's gone."

Shaka gazed through the trees. "No matter," she said.

Before them in the distance stood a cottage.

As they came nearer, they discovered that a series of ropes connected many of the trees and ran all the way to the front door. They approached the cottage—and heard a violin.

"There is your music," said Shaka.

"No, it's not the same," said Laney. "Same instrument maybe, but it sounds much different."

By now Shaka had removed the arrow from her crossbow and slung the strap of the bow back over her shoulder.

She stepped up to the front door and knocked.

RAYLA AND MAESTRO

No answer. Shaka knocked again. The music stopped, replaced by the sound of approaching footsteps.

The door opened, revealing a man pleasant to behold yet blessed with the wisdom of time. He stared straight ahead as if his eyes were locked upon a distant horizon. A woman came up behind him—fair skinned with honey-brown hair. Her years lay upon her with an elegant grace. She held a violin in one hand and a bow in the other.

"I *see* we have guests," said the man, emphasizing the word "see." "I *see*?—yes, well you need not laugh when I jest, but it may lighten your heart to do so. I am Maestro, and this is the beautiful Rayla, beautiful even for those who cannot see."

"Please come in," said Rayla. "Who are these who walk on four legs?"

"Tak and Gallia," said Shaka, "the most faithful companions I shall ever know."

"Then it will be our pleasure to meet them," said Maestro.

They entered the rustic cottage, not unlike Shaka's home with its sparse furnishings and warm fireplace glow.

In the middle of the room a large easel held a partially finished painting. "Do you enjoy art?" Maestro asked, turning his head toward Laney.

"I . . . think so," said Laney, not knowing but wanting to be polite.

Maestro moved toward the canvas, feeling the stool in front of it. He picked up a paintbrush. "Half a moment, if you please," he said, "and I shall set aside my painting for the day." He put his left hand at the bottom corner of the

A woman came up behind him—fair skinned with honey-brown hair.

canvas, as if that would enable him to understand where everything lay upon it. Then he leaned forward, so close that his nose nearly touched the glistening artwork. He moved his head from side to side, and up and down, all the while fidgeting with his brush as if restraining it. Then with a flick of his fingers and a twist of his wrist, he did his work—a half dozen quick strokes of brown. He leaned back to reveal a prancing deer.

"Wow!" said Laney. "How do you do that?"

"Practice—like anything else," said Maestro. "My sight is trapped in an ever-darkening tunnel, but my mind is free." Maestro nodded to himself. "Use what you have, and sometimes find a better way."

"Indeed," said Rayla with a laugh as clear and bright as rain in a rainbow.

"Rayla's music seeds my thoughts, awakens my imagination," said Maestro. He waved his hand as if he were conducting an orchestra. "But I am forgetting my manners," he continued. "Lay down your loads and I shall lay down my brush, and we shall all dine together."

Shaka and Laney dropped their gear, and Rayla set her violin in its place on a soft cloth.

"The paths seldom lead here," said Rayla, "and you are our first visitors in many a year. What brings you to our home?"

"We journey to find the clearing where dreams and visions become real and great deeds are possible. Do you know of such a place?"

"We know of the stories, and anything is possible in the West Woods," Rayla replied. "Even here you may find that your dreams have meaning beyond the simple wanderings of the mind. I dreamt of visitors from afar, and here you have arrived."

"My dreams don't make any sense," said Laney. "At least not the ones I can remember."

"Patience," said Maestro, leaning toward Laney to give her his full attention. "Life and dreams are like the start of a painting—brushstrokes that call for more layers to tell a tale—a tale whose meaning, even at the end, escapes all but the keenest of minds. Heed your dreams."

"Pray tell what you seek," said Rayla, "and we shall share what wisdom we have."

"I seek to end that which haunts the West Woods," said Shaka. "I seek to stop whatever drives the wolves against us. You perchance have a power that keeps the black fog away—how else can you live so deep in the West Woods?"

"All who live in this world have powers," said Rayla. "For Maestro and me, our power is here in this place we call home, and yes, neither the black fog nor the wolves have ever come to challenge us. But our power does not extend beyond the nearest trees. Two paths once led here, but both have long since shifted away—or worse. Maestro and I fear that what shifts to unknown places is not the paths but our home!" She paused for a moment, as if surprised by her own words. "The trees I see from our window remain the same," she explained, "but beyond that the woods seem to change, as if the winds carry us away to ever more distant lands. Sometimes I see a path through the trees tempting us to venture beyond where we know—but we dare not leave our home." A tear rolled down Rayla's cheek, and she wiped it away. "We raised our son, Braegon, here," she said. "Over the years Braegon became one with the Woods, learning its ways like no other. As a boy becoming a young man, he challenged himself by exploring the Woods, at times against our wishes. He braved the shifting paths, such were his skills. But one day he did not return, and ever since, we have questioned whether the paths alone shift or whether our home may wander as well. For we trust that Braegon's skills can see him through any hardships of the West Woods, and we know that he will never give up trying to return home. So you see we cannot leave this house for fear that Braegon will finally find his way back after we are no longer here."

"Braegon is one of the lost children of the Woods—lost but not gone," said Maestro.

"Men and boys, women and girls, sometimes disappear into the Woods," Rayla explained, "and while some may have been taken by the wolves, there are those, like Braegon, who can defend themselves and live off the land. We believe that Braegon and others wander alone but not without hope, and so we continue to wait for his return."

"Braegon has been gone for many winters, but a mother and father never give up hope," said Maestro. "Someday he will return. I see him in my dreams, and he is searching for us. Perhaps the coming of the syzygy will help him find us. This syzygy shall bestow powers and gifts to those who believe in its magic, and Braegon will use that to his advantage. We shall set out candles as the syzygy approaches, and perhaps Braegon will see the lights for real or in his dreams. Perhaps the candles will guide him back to us." Rayla hugged Maestro, and the warmth of their embrace seemed to fill the room. Then Rayla turned again to Shaka and Laney.

"Maestro and I have no magic to aid in your quest," she said. "All we can offer is food, a place to stay for this night, and what little wisdom we possess."

"Your hospitality is more aid than we could have hoped to receive," said Shaka.

Rayla smiled and nodded. "Perhaps our chance meeting is more than chance. I shall take it as a sign of better times to come. Now tell me, how are you prepared for your quest?"

"I have the arrows crafted in the older days and passed down from father to son, and mother to daughter—the arrows of Protection, Destiny, and Wrath," Shaka declared.

"Protection and Destiny will serve you well," said Maestro. "Where Wrath is present, misfortune often leads and follows."

"I come prepared with all that might serve me," said Shaka.

Then Rayla said, "These arrows you tell were passed down from father to son, and mother to daughter, but if these are indeed the arrows you believe, there is more to the story than that. They once belonged to Graigon of Peltston.

They disappeared just before the fall of Peltston and Buroakville, some claiming that Dalida took them as a gift. How they fell into the line of your family is a mystery. 'Tis often said that power seeks those with the strength to wield it, and such may be true of your arrows."

"That I know not," said Shaka.

"Have you the crimson arrow?" asked Rayla.

"Yes."

"Then you are prepared," said Rayla. "I am sorry."

"Sorry?" said Laney. "What do you mean?"

"Has Shaka not told you?" exclaimed Rayla. "'*Where evil lurks and has no fear, none shall dare to venture near, save one with blessed arrow red, to pierce the darkness and the dread—and leave this world behind.'* The crimson arrow will not suffer itself to be left behind in the quiver. When the need arises, it will find Shaka's hand, and it will prove victorious, but you shall return alone."

"But anything can happen, right? Nobody knows," said Laney.

"Some who are wise would agree," Maestro mused.

"Show me the arrow," said Rayla.

Shaka retrieved the arrow from her quiver and handed it to Rayla. The evening light had begun to fade, so Rayla lit a lantern and held the arrow close to the light.

"This *is* the crimson arrow foretold," she said as she turned the shaft in her hand. "The thread is braided in strands of four. The shaft has four marks here, and beneath the feathers are the letters AICZ. The initials of the wise from the older days."

"Z as in Zelfore?" asked Laney.

"The names have been lost to time," said Rayla. "Only the initials remain. But this arrow is the one. Even without the initials, I could tell—'tis cold to the touch even in the warmth of my home. This arrow was crafted before the black fog first came. It has a power, but it commands a price. You shall use it only one time."

"I fear not what I must do," declared Shaka.

"What about the other arrows?" asked Laney. "Can't she just use the other arrows? What about their powers?"

"Doubt not that the other arrows will serve you on your journey," explained Rayla, "but if the prophecy holds true, then only the crimson arrow will accomplish your task."

"Prophesies are not commandments," Maestro interjected. "You can turn away at any time. This task may fall upon the next generation or many generations beyond."

"There will be no next generation for me," Shaka replied. "This is my quest, and I shall not turn back."

"Very well," said Rayla, "but be forewarned that the West Woods does not suffer anyone to tread through its depths, no matter how lightly. Your presence will be felt, and resisted."

Shaka nodded and wrapped her cloak about her.

"Shall I put more wood on the fire?" Rayla asked.

"Your home is most comfortable and your hospitality most gracious. I shiver not from lack of heat but from a wound that festers. It is a burden I must bear," said Shaka.

"Show me," said Rayla.

Shaka lifted her sleeve, now stained and crusted yellow and brown on the underside. The wound had worsened since morning. The cut that Shaka had made to release the infection had swollen, and the rotting ooze flowed heavier than before.

"You have cut the wound," observed Rayla.

"I deemed it would help."

"Your wound is foul," said Rayla. "You were wise to open it with a clean blade."

"Almost clean," said Shaka. "A black stain is upon it, from I know not what."

"Vines!" exclaimed Laney, remembering the great arch. "They grabbed me, and I cut them. They bled black."

"I cannot say," said Shaka.

"Black-veined vines," said Rayla. "Another peril of the West Woods. That alone could foul a wound. I shall clean your blade after I have a closer look at this wound."

"It grows worse with each passing day," Shaka admitted. "I fear my strength shall be gone when I need it most."

"In the West Woods, the syzygy has much power—not all of it good. The closer you get to the heart of the West Woods and the time of the syzygy, the weaker you shall become. The bite of the West Woods wolf is an ill fate indeed for one who would stand against the packs."

"If my strength wanes," said Shaka, "then my will shall become ever stronger."

"The prophecy is not yours to command and perhaps not yours to fulfill," said Rayla. "Even the wisest of the wise cannot foresee its end. But where there is a will undaunted, there is hope. Show me the blade used to open your wound."

Shaka unfastened her knife and presented it to Rayla. Rayla drew it from its sheath, and her eyes widened. "Such a blade I have not seen in all my years." she said. "This gives me hope. How came you upon such a blade?"

"My father gave it to me, but I know not how it came into his care."

"This blade was forged in the younger days," Rayla declared. "I know not what charms it may possess, but to be sure, it has a higher purpose. May it serve you well in your time of need." She inspected the engraved markings and the black streak along both sides. "Such a blade should not bear the indignity of a stain. After I bathe your wound, I shall tend to this." She laid the knife on the table and went to fetch warm water.

She cleaned the wound, and then poured honey over it. "There is no cure for the bite of a West Woods wolf," she said, "but this will help. 'Tis made from the nectar of the glamendorn tree. Its healing power is potent." She placed a clean cloth over the wound.

"It no longer burns like fire," said Shaka. "Your skill as a healer is great indeed."

"Your body is strong," said Rayla, "and your spirit as well." Then she turned to Laney. "There is more to you than meets the eye. Do you not agree, Maestro?"

"That even a blind man can see," he replied. "What tale have you to tell? But wait half a moment, and Rayla shall bring food and drink. Even the best stories tell better with a hearty meal."

Rayla left and returned with bowls of stew, a rose-colored drink, and a jug of water. To Laney, it looked like a feast. There was plenty for Tak and Gallia, too.

When their thirsts were quenched and the meal well underway, Maestro repeated his question to Laney.

"I have no story," she said. "I only remember the past several days, starting at Shaka's home—and now we're here."

"No memory?" Maestro said with a tone of wonderment. "No burdens from the past? What an extraordinary gift."

"Gift? I don't think so."

"But it is!" Maestro bellowed. "Now you can be anybody. You can start anew and live the life you choose." Maestro nodded a few times. "And you get the riches of time."

"Time?" said Laney.

"Yes, time. The older we get, the faster it flies—but not for you. I blink, and a day goes by—but for you each day must seem like an eternity of experiences."

"I don't know," said Laney. "I never really thought about it."

"Some believe that time is as steady as a mountain, that the paths of the sun and the moon are endlessly the same," Maestro said. "But time is cunning, and most unkind. It slows when we watch and then runs when we look the other way. It all but stops to prolong our suffering and then hastens for our greatest joys, stealing precious moments."

"Time is time," said Laney. She did not want to be contradictory, but she disliked the idea that something as simple as time wasn't simple at all. Then she thought for a moment. "Except maybe when we dream," she mused, half wondering where that thought might have come from.

"Oh, what a gift you have," Maestro repeated. "And if you should regain your memory, the wisdom from this experience may be the most valuable gift of all."

"That's what I want—to remember," said Laney. "Shaka believes that I will remember everything when we get to the clearing."

"Perhaps," said Maestro, "but how will you get to the clearing? Can you use your powers?"

"I don't have any powers—at least not that I remember."

"That is most unfortunate." Maestro tapped his foot several times, as if that might summon the answers he sought. "No one should venture to the heart of the West Woods unaided. You must harness your powers, command the forces that surround you. You have such abilities. Do you have a wand?"

"What, like a magic wand?"

"No, a wand is not magical," Maestro explained. "'Tis the person who uses the wand that gives it power. My brush is just a useless stick to most people, but you see what I can do with it. The power starts in my mind and then flows through my hand, through the brush, and onto the canvas."

"So how do I get a wand, and then what do I do with it?" asked Laney.

"Any stick will do," Maestro replied. "Even your walking stick—that is all you need. Think of it as a wizard's staff, and it will become more than a simple stick —you will see."

"I don't see how," said Laney. *I don't believe in such things,* she thought. *How can something impossible work if I don't even believe it?*

"You must believe," said Maestro, sensing her thoughts, "because that is where it all begins. Is it so difficult to believe that you have hidden powers?"

"I don't know. Almost everything about me seems hidden," Laney replied.

"If you do not call forth your powers, then surely someone else will find a way to summon them," said Maestro, "perhaps not to your liking. Your powers will either aid you or enslave you—master them!"

Laney wanted to believe in the impossible. "I'll try," she said, "but then what happens? How will I know what I can do?"

"Heed your dreams," Maestro advised. "Let them flow, and try to understand. But remember, your dreams happen on their own and not necessarily for your benefit. Sometimes they can weaken resolve or lead you astray. It takes a keen mind to use them properly."

"Much of my mind is blank," Laney said, and she wondered how she could possibly make sense of dreams without more knowledge.

"Dreams are like brushstrokes," said Maestro. "Better to start with a blank canvas." He raised his cup and nodded to Rayla and then to each of his guests. "'Tis a pleasure to share food and drink with such company. May your journeys lead to new beginnings."

They ate and drank their fill, and the dinner conversation turned to lighter matters. Shaka shared stories of her youth, and Rayla told tales of wonder about the West Woods before the black fog. Laney found it all quite enchanting, but she had difficulty keeping her eyes open, and more than once her head nodded down and snapped back up, only to start nodding again.

"The hour is late, and at least one of our guests is weary," said Rayla as Maestro finished the last of his drink. "We have but modest accommodations for guests, but you shall be safe from the wind and the cold."

She led her guests to a small room in the back. There she put her hand on Laney's shoulder and said, "Dream well so that you might know the dangers that await."

Elzikon

Laney fell asleep almost as soon as she lay down. So deep was her sleep that even the darkness disappeared, and her mind became a void, a blank canvas for . . . shattering glass. As the thousand sparkling crystals filled Laney's mind, they began to float and change into . . . brown leaves falling—closer, bigger, until each leaf seemed the size of a winter coat. Thicker and faster they fell, and then, like a curtain at a theater, they parted and revealed . . . a squirrel, close up, looking right at Laney.

Laney sat up with a start. Like a child who awakens from a dream and doesn't understand that it's a dream, she cast her gaze about the room looking for the squirrel. The squirrel had something to say, or do, or somehow make sense of her thoughts—but how? And now it was gone.

"Your dreams have fled," said Shaka. "'Tis daybreak, and there is food on the table."

Laney's mind cleared, revealing her morning hunger, and she arose for breakfast. She joined Rayla and Maestro at the table, and they exchanged pleasantries as Laney devoured all that was offered.

When Shaka joined them after readying the packs, Rayla spoke: "You have little more than two days' journey before the syzygy. I have never ventured to the heart of the West Woods, nor do I know any who have tried. But if such a journey is possible, now is the time. Heed your dreams, but beware—visions can guide you, or they can deceive you. What you see and hear and what is real may be difficult to tell."

"I think that yesterday I heard something that wasn't there," Laney shared, finally saying what had been nagging at her since the previous day. "I heard music that led us here, but I don't think it was your music. And I think maybe it's not the first time that I heard it—but I don't know—it sounded so familiar."

"You would not have heard my music from afar," Rayla said. "I think you have felt the magic of the Woods. I take this as a good sign. My wisdom in these matters is not great, but I think you should follow the music if you hear it again. You are fortunate to be here this day, and whatever led you here might help you again."

Maestro nodded in agreement.

"I wish you could come with us," Laney said to Rayla.

Rayla sighed and put her hand to her chest where a crystal hung from the fine chain around her neck. "I shall wait for Braegon," she said. "Besides, my powers are no match for what you seek to face. No, Maestro and I shall remain here until such time as our son returns, or our hearts cease to beat. But if the prophecy holds true, you shall not need my help, for neither Rayla nor Maestro is mentioned in the tales and songs of old."

"I believe the words of the prophecy," said Shaka. "With every passing day I become more certain of what is meant to be."

"And now you must resume your journey," said Rayla.

"Yes," said Shaka, "though I am sorry to leave such hospitality behind. Our journey cannot wait."

And so after brief, heartfelt good-byes, the travelers headed on their way.

In spite of her fever, Shaka led Laney and the dogs at a brisk pace. But when the terrain began to rise, Shaka leaned heavily on her stick. They came to the crest of a hill, and Shaka stopped for a brief rest.

"We have come far, and as quickly as I had hoped," she said. "We are living inside a tale that we shall bring to an end, and no one could ask for more. I feel my destiny as sure as I breathe. Your role is a mystery, but we shall see."

Shaka rose and unstrapped her knife. "Take this blade," she said. "It is a fitting weapon for a sorceress. Rayla has cleaned it, and it shines like fine silver." She fastened the knife at Laney's side. "May it serve you well!"

Laney wanted to refuse, believing any weapon would serve them better in Shaka's hands. But she found herself saying, "Thank you," and as she placed her hand upon the hilt, she couldn't help but think, *My place is beside Shaka, and Tak, and Gallia, wherever that might lead.*

Soon they resumed their journey, but the day brought with it dark thoughts for Laney. With each step, her anxiety grew. Mostly she worried about Shaka. Shaka's mind seemed to be elsewhere whenever Laney spoke to her, as if Laney's voice came as a surprise each time. And Shaka's neck now bent forward as if the task of holding her head erect strained it to its limits.

Throughout the day the sun shone favorably upon them as it seemed to weave its way through the trees, and in its wake the cold seemed to retreat. Nonetheless, Shaka shivered.

Gallia stayed close to her master, often looking up at her as if to say, "Lean on me." Shaka made frequent stops to sniff the air and read the wind—she seemed less sure of herself than before. So when she stopped yet again, Laney was not surprised until she saw that they both stood at the edge of a wide trail.

"We found this path just as the need arose," said Shaka. "We may hope that good fortune is upon us, but we must be cautious. My instincts tell me this path was not here yesterday."

"If it's going where we are, does it matter?"

"We shall see," said Shaka.

The path took them in an ever-westerly direction, across a small stream, and over rolling hills, until it split in front of a centuries-old fir tree standing like a sentinel.

"Another choice," said Shaka. "You choose, but this time you must truly choose."

Laney blushed. "Okay—how?"

"I cannot say, except that music guided you once before. If you cannot hear the music, search for it in your mind. Perhaps the memory of it will help you decide."

Laney stood before the tree at the split in the path, took a deep breath, and closed her eyes. She imagined the music—not just the notes, but the way it made her giddy with hope. She felt a tingle go down her back like cool water on a summer day. And then, though her eyes remained closed, the tree appeared. And just as she wondered how that could be, it came crashing toward her. She lurched to the side.

"Steady!" said Shaka, catching Laney as she stumbled. "I see you have chosen—most definitely." Gallia bounded toward the chosen path.

"I don't know what happened," Laney stammered. "The tree came at me, and I tried to get out of the way, and then it felt like I was asleep and waking up at the same time."

"Your powers are awakening to your command," Shaka proclaimed. "They shall take getting used to."

The path they chose wound its way through the trees, rarely revealing itself more than a stone's throw ahead. At times Gallia scouted ahead as Shaka seemed to struggle, stumbling more than once. Only her walking stick kept her from falling.

Suddenly the dogs bolted down the path, and Shaka charged after them.

Laney raced to catch up. She rounded a bend, and there before her lay an animal. Dead. A deer more massive than any Laney could have imagined or would have remembered. Its great rack spanned the width of the path.

Shaka knelt before the fallen deer and put her hand upon its chest. "I knew this buck," she said. "A jewel of his kind. Such dignity and grace. Many a time over the years we chanced upon each other, and sometimes I would follow to learn his ways."

"Did the wolves do that?" Laney asked.

"Yes," replied Shaka. "These wolves no longer obey the laws of their nature, the order of the forest. Packs once kept one another in check, but with the change in the West Woods the packs began banding together, and these wolves pay no heed to the time of day. They no longer kill because they must eat; they now kill without reason. And even the great bucks with their mastery of the woods are at risk. This is not the first buck I have seen left to rot. But this one grieves me more than any other."

The sun arced overhead in what seemed to Laney like an endless day. "I feel like I've been walking in my sleep," she murmured.

"This day grows short," said Shaka, her head bowed. "We must see it through. We have come far, and we shall have a full night to rest—tonight and one more, and then we shall reach our destination."

"Our destination—I'll give anything to remember. I know what Maestro said, but I need to know who I am."

"Have no memories returned?"

"Nothing," said Laney. "Just a vague sense of something, like when you wake up and know you had a dream but can't remember it."

"Maybe that is a beginning," said Shaka.

The trail narrowed, forcing the travelers to walk in single file. The trees seemed to huddle closer together, and in the failing light both Shaka and Laney stumbled on roots that crisscrossed the path. Finally Shaka said, "Darkness grows, though the day remains, and the air smells stale—something is amiss."

Shaka readied her crossbow. She sniffed the air for a scent hiding beneath the musty odor of the forest. Gallia and Tak stared through the trees. Someone was there!

"Hello there!" Shaka called, and in answer a man came forward and stepped onto the path. The hide of a bear stretched from his shoulders and back down to his feet, and two fox pelts encircled his neck. His left hand hung at his side, absent parts of the two smallest fingers, and a scar stretched from his forehead to his ear. Though his hair and beard had grown long and gray, he stood tall and straight, towering above Shaka and Laney. His right hand rested upon a hunting knife fastened at his side by a deerskin belt. A bow and quiver hung from his shoulder.

"Our meeting is fortunate, and not entirely by chance," said the stranger. "Are you not the keeper of the arrows?"

"That you can see," said Shaka. "And you have one of mine." She glanced at the stranger's quiver, with one arrow different from the others: an arrow with black feathers. "You have been following us—what is your purpose?"

"You need my help," said the man. "You are wounded. I see the stain upon your sleeve, and I can smell it as well."

"Then you have a keen nose," Shaka replied. "What else have you to say?"

"I am Elzikon, and I have been keeping watch as the day of the prophecy approaches. Fate has brought us together."

"These times and the coming of the syzygy are no secret from one who knows the West Woods. What is your business with us?"

The man smiled, as one might when dealing with small children who need to feel comforted. "I am here to help," he replied, but his voice lacked the ring of truth, and his furtive glances seemed calculating rather than inquisitive.

"To help us or yourself?" said Shaka.

"Both," Elzikon replied. "The prophecy must be fulfilled, and there is only one way for that to happen." He reached inside his tunic where it hung loose from his neck, and pulled out a necklace. He held it for them to see, and the

. . . a scar stretched from his forehead to his ear.

stone at the center glistened as if it had an internal light of many colors. "Behold, the Stone of Agashore, the great protector! It bestows courage in the face of fear, strength for the weary, wit for the outwitted, healing for the wounded, and good fortune beyond hope. Surely you know the tales, and to look upon it is to know it is real. This stone has seen me safe through time and events beyond your reckoning, and it can do the same for you. This stone is what you need to fulfill the prophecy!"

Shaka's eyes widened as she looked upon it.

"You believe you travel with the Sorceress from the West, yet she knows not so herself. She wields no powers to aid in your quest. How do I know this? I know much from my travels and my years wearing the Stone of Agashore. The prophecy is doomed—unless you have a helping hand."

Elzikon glanced at Laney, and then back to Shaka. "Give me your albatross that knows not how to fly," he said, "and I shall teach her to soar, to be the Sorceress from the West, and you shall have what you need to fulfill the prophecy—the Stone of Agashore. The trade for this Stone is the only helping hand you shall receive from this girl!"

And then Laney remembered the words of Maestro, that if she did not master her powers, someone else would, and not to her liking. She felt the blood rush from her head. She leaned on her walking stick with trembling hands, and looked to Shaka. But Shaka kept her steely eyes locked on Elzikon.

Elzikon removed the necklace and placed it on a boulder that lay nearby. "Test it for yourself," he said. "Surely you know how."

Shaka hesitated, but then picked up a rock the size of a large melon and approached the boulder where the necklace lay. She raised the rock above her head, and with all her might brought the rock down upon the glistening gem. With a sound like thunder, the rock shattered, and the boulder beneath split in two as if sliced by a sword. And there upon the earth between the two halves of the boulder, the gem lay unscathed, sparkling even in the shadow of the broken rock. Elzikon reached and picked it up, and held it out for Shaka to see. She gazed upon the stone and said, "Indeed this is the storied stone, and its value is more than any can say. I must question why you offer such a trade."

"In your heart and mind you know the answer," said Elzikon. "This stone, and all the lesser stones, run their course for whoever bears them. At first the magic is beyond the wildest of dreams, but then it fades for the one who wears it, as if Agashore grows weary of serving a single master. But a new master will command the full powers of Agashore, and those are mighty indeed. I have gained all that I ever shall from this stone—it is worth much more to you than it is to me. And this girl is of no use to you, but I know how to awaken her powers. I can teach her, and she shall serve the West Woods that you care to protect."

"I have no doubt that she would serve you—and I do not doubt that this is the Stone of Agashore," Shaka declared. "I could use such aid as I go where I must. Nevertheless, there may be more than one way to any destination, and who is to say what is best? I shall not forsake my companion for a chance to walk the easy path."

"Then you are a fool," scoffed Elzikon, his face twisted with rage. "Your quest is doomed, and the West Woods shall fall beyond the reach of any prophecy."

He turned to Laney and softened his tone. "Fair Sorceress, do you not long to know who you are and what you can do? Has not this woman failed to answer your questions or satisfy your needs? You have a purpose, if you so choose, far greater than the paths you wander. Come with me, and discover for yourself. I alone can protect you!"

Laney's heart pounded. She put a hand to her chest. Her necklace—the Sun Stone. It pressed against her skin. A warmth ran through her. Her mind became clear, unafraid.

She turned to Shaka, and their eyes met, and now she realized what she must do. "I will go with Shaka," she said.

"Fools—both of you!" cried Elzikon. "The dullards of Tarzetta are the downfall of the West Woods and beyond. I offered you a fair deal to save yourselves when I could have taken by force that which I want. Your arrows are useless against me so long as I wield the Stone of Agashore!" He held the great stone aloft and then placed its chain around his neck, and he seemed to grow in stature as the stone lay upon his chest.

"If what you say is true, you would not have offered a deal," said Shaka as she raised her crossbow. "Do you dare test the waning power of your stone against the arrows of the prophecy? With the power of your stone, you can no doubt sense the lesser crystals that we wear—lesser but not without power. My companion wears the Sun Stone, and neither that stone nor she will ever be taken by force."

"You think yourself clever," Elzikon retorted, "but when you find yourself face to face with the wolves in the black fog, what will you do then? A thousand archers will not stop the hordes that will come for you. They will tear your flesh and gnaw your bones—and they are especially fond of dogs!"

Tak barked, and Gallia growled.

"Be gone!" said Shaka. "And be grateful that we do not take from you what we need." She aimed her crossbow as a warning, and Elzikon stepped back, shaking with rage. He spat at their feet and then hastened away. Shaka called out, "The prophecy tells naught of the name of Elzikon."

Shaka kept her eye on him until he disappeared. "He will think twice before troubling us again," she said, "but he may not have seen the last of me. If ever the prophecy is fulfilled, I shall seek the Stone of Agashore and learn how it came to Elzikon."

The travelers continued their journey, and soon the sun danced upon the horizon. They came to a dry stream bed, and Shaka led them alongside to a point where rushing waters from ages past had carved the rolling land.

"This will do," Shaka said as they stood beneath an earthen overhang. "I shall build fires in an arc around us, and Tak and Gallia shall share the night's watch. I must save my strength for the day."

Gallia went with Shaka to gather tinder for a series of fires. Laney found a comfortable spot to lie down, and Tak came to sit beside her—but rather than face Laney, he turned toward the surrounding woods. Laney could tell he was looking, listening, and smelling for any signs of danger.

A Flash of Anger

Dreams are the whitecaps in a sea of reality, their froth mixing with the surf, turning to spray, vanishing into the sea air.

In the void of dreamless sleep, Laney heard a screech, as of a raptor descending upon prey. Then a vision formed, a black shape coming toward her, rimmed by the light of the sun. She felt a whirlwind of wings as a shadow descended—and then a blow so massive the very impact separated her mind from her body. The light of the sun gave way to darkness, and then with a start, she awoke.

She sat bolt upright and turned toward the fire, where Tak and Gallia sat peering into the darkness. Laney took a deep breath, welcoming the chill of the air into her lungs. She watched the mist of her breath disappear into the night, and willed the last remnants of her dream to do the same—but they lingered.

I've heard that screech before, Laney thought, though she could not recall whether it came from another dream, the sound of the woods at night, or the depths of her lost memories. She lay back down, and more dreams came to haunt her sleep.

"Steady! Easy there—you are awake now," Shaka said as Laney flailed her arms, chasing away yet another dream. "You are too late to greet the dawn, but not too late for breakfast."

"You were . . . your bow was broken," said Laney, and before she could offer more, the dream escaped her thoughts.

"Not all that you dream is real," said Shaka.

Laney looked about to get her bearings. The trees stretched endlessly before her. Tak and Gallia were busy attending to their rations. By all appearances, this was the start of just another day. Still, Laney's heart raced and her hands trembled.

She put her hand to her chest and felt her necklace through the layers of clothing. If the Sun Stone enhanced her intuition, she couldn't tell.

She kept quiet as she ate and then readied to start the day's journey. Shaka, for her part, seemed content with the silence.

They turned their backs to the rising sun and began another day's trek. The hours passed without event, but Shaka and Laney both struggled. They stopped for food and rest at midday, but even then the forest seemed to drain their energy.

Toward day's end they happened upon a path, but the flat terrain gave way to a procession of hills and valleys. Laney began to feel that the forest toyed with them. She felt as though they were being watched, like ants that could be crushed at any moment. But instead of fear, she felt a growing determination to complete their journey.

Then a rock, half buried and hidden by leaves and snow, caught Laney's foot. She slammed onto the ground. As she picked herself up, she saw what had tripped her, and anger welled up inside her. She raised her stick high above her head and drove it into the rock with all the force she could muster.

The rock shattered. Laney and the dogs all jumped, but Shaka didn't flinch.

"Your powers are growing," she said. "That cannot be denied." She picked up a piece of the rock the size of her fist. "Remember this rock the next time you must use your powers. This stone is as hard as any in the great mountains, and you broke it with a mere flash of anger. You are indeed the Sorceress from the West, and your powers shall prevail—you shall see."

Laney just looked at her stick and what was left of the rock.

Shaka stepped off the path and retrieved another rock, this one the size of a large melon. She dropped it at Laney's feet. "Again," she said.

Laney concentrated for a moment, then raised her stick and drove the point downward as hard as she could toward the rock. But in her excitement, she struck only a glancing blow. She felt her face turn red, but she gritted her teeth and raised the stick again. She slammed it with all her might—but the rock withstood the blow, and the stick vibrated so fiercely that her hands felt as if they had just been stung by bees.

With a yell, she dropped the stick. Shaka picked it up and handed it back. "Stone will not surrender to the strength of your arms or your stick. Summon your spirit—*that* will break this rock."

Laney reached deep to find the anger she had felt. It was gone. But as she concentrated, she found something else—a confidence, a faith—and when she touched upon it, it seemed to spread throughout her body. She raised the stick again, and with one smooth, sure stroke, rained it down upon the rock. With a sound like thunder, the rock shattered into pebbles and dust.

Laney smiled. "Let's find some more rocks," she said.

Shaka laughed. "You can practice later. Now I must find a place for us to pass the night. Come, we shall leave the path and look nearby. Where there are hills, sometimes there are caves. We shall look for one."

Whether by skill or instinct, Shaka could read the land and knew where to look for shelter. She led them along the floor of a valley, and around two of the larger hills, and found a cave just as the sun balanced at the end of the sky.

"Good fortune is with us." Shaka crouched to step inside the opening. "'Tis much larger in here," she said, her voice echoing through the cavern. "I shall build fires outside, enough to protect us. Eat what you will, and then sleep long and deep. Tomorrow is the syzygy, and we shall both need our strength and our wits."

Attack in the Night

As the travelers slept soundly and flames danced amidst the blackness of the night, Tak stirred. His nose wrinkled, and suddenly he sat bolt upright. Gallia jumped to her feet, and both dogs barked an urgent warning. Shaka leaped from the cave, her crossbow aimed into the dark.

"Come Tak, Gallia!—yes, I smell them too—wolves, lots of wolves, all around. Stay here, steady now. I am ready!"

No one could cock and fire a crossbow faster that Shaka, but a simultaneous attack by many wolves would be a difficult trial for her skills. Her head spun from fever and her arm throbbed, both threatening her aim.

Now a gold-threaded arrow lay notched and ready. Wolf eyes glowed, circling beyond the fire. Shaka pulled the trigger.

The arrow flew past the flames. Straight and true—a wolf dropped dead. But others came with a vengeance. Shaka let fly another arrow. And another. Two more wolves dropped. One landed in the fire—flames and embers shot high into the night sky. Howls in the darkness—two wolves came. Tak and Gallia leaped forward. Shaka fired again. One wolf dropped. The other came like a beast possessed.

Tak and Gallia stood firm, teeth barred, ready for battle. The wolf, in a tremendous bound, leaped over the dogs. It came for Shaka's throat. Her crossbow only half cocked, she raised it. No time—the arrow flew.

At half force, the arrow found its mark. The wolf tumbled at her feet—dead before it hit the ground.

Shaka fitted another arrow. Violet. She stepped toward the fire. A rage swelled within her such that even the flames seemed to bend away from her presence. She fired, and then loaded and fired again. The wolves drew back. Shaka charged past the bodies of the fallen. And there she stood between the two largest fires, aglow in the red of the firelight and the flush of rage and fever. She stepped past the flames, and her shadow stretched forward until swallowed by darkness. Then she let loose a battle cry more thunderous than the greatest storms the forest had ever known. The remaining wolves fled, and there Shaka stood, her chest heaving in and out as she caught her breath.

Laney grabbed her stick and came running from the cave. When she reached Shaka, the huntress turned and nodded.

"They are gone," she said, "but I am glad that you have come."

"Will they come again?" asked Laney. She would face wolves with her stick, with or without any special powers.

"I think not," said Shaka. "They are reckless, but they lost more of their number than they bargained for."

Shaka threw more tinder onto the fires, and then she and Laney returned to the cave. Tak and Gallia once again stood guard at the entrance.

As Laney closed her eyes to welcome sleep, she felt an unexpected calm, a sense that she did belong on this journey and that she indeed was playing a part in a tale greater than her own.

Shaka remained awake. As much as she needed sleep, the fight with the wolves had given her a second wind. She unslung her quiver and counted the arrows—somehow they would have to be enough.

Strange Encounters

"Shhh," Shaka said. "Wake up—it is time. Our destiny is near. I can feel it."

"My dreams," said Laney. "Wolves everywhere."

"Come—we must go. 'Tis later than you think. Tak, Gallia, stay close this day. We shall all need one another."

Shaka sniffed the air and looked at the sky in all directions. "Snow and wind have not hindered us yet," she said, "but today may be different—too many clouds. We may be facing a storm before the day grows old. We must hurry."

They readied themselves, then headed into their final day, the day of the syzygy. Tak and Laney, side by side, followed behind Shaka and Gallia as they headed west out of the valley.

"There will be no paths where we go today," said Shaka, "but I sense we are close, and we shall arrive before the syzygy."

"How will we know when we're there?" asked Laney.

"As sure as you know when the sun shines or when the rain falls, you will know that you have arrived. We shall enter a clearing, and we shall both know that it is the one. You shall find who you are, and together we shall fulfill the prophecy and restore tranquility to the West Woods."

Their march that day began without event, Shaka picking her way through the maze of trees with confidence even in the face of her waning strength. But the trek became more difficult as the day wore on. The trees grew so thick that the sun's rays became lost to the travelers below. An eerie darkness settled onto the forest, hiding gnarled roots, clingy vines, and deep ruts.

"We must rest, if only a short while," said Shaka. "We shall travel all the faster thereafter."

They lay together, using their packs as pillows. Tak came to lie beside Laney, and she rested her arm on his powerful back. She closed her eyes, inviting sleep—her breathing slowed, aches and pains faded. But just as she drifted off to the world of dreams, she heard a swirling of wind.

Shaka jumped to her feet. "Who are you?" she demanded, an arrow already fitted and cocked.

"Do you not know?" a man replied, stepping from the trees and wrestling against the wind to tame his cape.

"Zelfore!" exclaimed Laney.

"Right you are. Of course I knew you would be here. Though time whisks all save me toward an uncertain end, this moment at least I know."

"Then you know what will happen with the syzygy?" asked Laney.

"Events flow like water," said Zelfore. "They find a way. Fill one crack, and water finds or makes another. Sometimes I fill cracks, but will that keep the dam from breaking? No one can say."

"Why are you here?" asked Shaka.

"I have come to say the time is nigh. If the prophecy is what you seek, now you must awake."

And as Zelfore uttered his last words, Laney realized that he was but a dream. Zelfore offered a tight-lipped smile, spun around, and with a swirl of snow and darkness, disappeared.

Laney opened her eyes. As she sat up, so too did Shaka.

"We must begin our final journey," said Shaka. They exchanged glances, but neither spoke of their dreams or why they had awoken at the same time.

Upon hearing their master's voice, Tak and Gallia stood up, ready to follow.

Both Laney and Shaka felt surprisingly refreshed. Shaka led them much quicker than before. The hills flattened, and vines gave way. Trees thinned, letting light filter through the canopy.

"Were you sleeping before when we stopped?" Laney finally asked.

"Yes—I did not mean to, but I must have fallen asleep, because I remember waking."

"Did you have a dream?" asked Laney.

"I do not remember."

They hastened to make up for lost time, but as the sun climbed, so too did Shaka's fever.

"My pack is light," said Laney. "I can carry more."

Shaka shook her head. "My pack is not what burdens me. The fever is taking its toll, but you need not worry—my will is strong."

Tak and Gallia trotted ahead, finding the best ways through the maze of trees and brush, and scouting for dangers. Laney stayed close behind Shaka.

Soon Shaka's pace slowed, and Laney felt thankful because she, too, began to struggle. Her knees ached, and as she wondered *why now?* she realized that it wasn't just her knees. Her hips and ankles felt weak and tight.

Gallia whimpered, and Shaka held up a hand, motioning all to stop.

"Gallia is limping, and my legs feel like they're frozen and on fire at the same time," said Shaka.

Then, without warning, Shaka fitted an arrow and raised her crossbow. Through the trees, someone stood peering at them, close enough that Shaka or the dogs should have been alerted by sound or smell.

"Show yourself!" Shaka demanded, but whoever lurked behind that tree stood still and silent. Shaka moved to get a clear shot. She stepped past one tree and then another. Her aim locked on the stranger.

"Speak before I loose an arrow that will pierce your heart! Who are you who spies upon us?"

But the stranger remained silent and frozen—and naked! A woman, as pale as snow, stood expressionless before her. Shaka approached and lowered her crossbow. And then through the trees she saw others, trapped in poses of an

"Show yourself!" Shaka demanded.

ordinary nature, some standing but most sitting or fallen onto the ground. Their expressions ranged from vacant to grim. Neither a hint of a smile nor a trace of joy graced any face, not even that of a child.

Laney and the dogs caught up with Shaka.

"The suffering on their faces is real," said Shaka. "Touch naught lest you invite the spell that is upon them."

Most of the figures were women, and many of them appeared to be elderly, as if old age had weakened their resistance to this curse. But there were also some younger ones, and Laney found herself drawn to a girl about her age who stared with a silent plea upon her lips, as if begging for rescue.

And then a memory stirred and Laney realized she had seen this face before —again and again, ever smaller—all the generations that would never be.

How can that be? she thought to herself—and to that she had no answer.

Sorrow welled up in Laney, and she wished that if she had just one special power, it would be to awaken the statues.

"We must go," said Shaka, interrupting her thoughts.

"There are dozens of them," said Laney, "or more."

"Yes, and there may be two more plus the dogs if we stay any longer." Shaka clenched and unclenched her hands, willing the stiff joints to move. "This curse lingers still. We must make haste!"

Shaka ran as best she could, and Laney chased after her, gritting her teeth. Her feet felt like bricks. Her lungs tightened, and she gasped for air. Her head spun. Her heart pounded—slower and slower, winding down.

Tak barked at Laney's side. Gallia limped behind. Shaka led them up an impossible hill, and then as they reached the crest, both she and Laney fell headfirst down the snowy slope. They and the dogs tumbled like logs, bouncing off trees all the way to the bottom of the hill. And there they lay, feeling nothing.

Braegon

Melting snow slid down Laney's face, tickling her cheek. She shook her head and sat up, feeling energy return to her body. She turned toward Shaka, who seemed to be making a similar recovery. Gallia stretched her legs while Tak paced back and forth.

"Those were real people!" Laney declared when she caught her breath.

"Long ago," said Shaka.

"What happened to their clothes?"

"Cloth and hides cannot withstand the tests of time," said Shaka. "Those people have been there for a time beyond reckoning. Not even the soles of their shoes remain—only stone which they have become, and some day that too will disappear."

Shaka and Laney both fell silent. Then Tak barked, and Shaka nodded. "Yes, we must move on." And so they left the stone people behind, their misfortune preserved for the ages—another unsolved mystery of the West Woods.

As they marched onward, the trees became thicker, and clouds blanketed the forest, blotting out any trace of the sun. The wind pushed back with each step forward, but Shaka's will drove them onward. Laney had never felt so tired, but she matched Shaka step for step.

Then suddenly everything changed for Laney. Her legs felt lighter. Her breath came easier. She felt an energy she had never known.

"We are nearing the heart of the West Woods," Shaka proclaimed. "Do you feel it?"

"I do."

"Like a spring day in the middle of winter."

"Day?" said Laney. "I can barely see anything." So thick were the trees that shadows hung like night upon the forest.

But where eyes might fail, the ears and noses of Tak and Gallia prevailed. Tak barked a warning, and instantly Shaka fitted an arrow. If Elzikon had returned, she was ready. Though the threat approached from deep within the shadows, Shaka's Destiny arrow would find its mark.

"Lower your weapon!" came a voice through the darkness. "I mean you no harm." The voice was not of Elzikon.

"Show yourself," Shaka commanded.

Approaching footsteps fell lightly with the skill of a hunter. Laney held her breath.

Then, as if the sun itself had parted the trees, a man clad in the pelts of wolves stepped before them. Young but grim he appeared in the stream of sunshine that fell upon him, as though his time in the Woods had taken a toll well beyond the count of years. Yet in spite of his weathered look, a shock of honey-brown hair and eyes as deep as a well made his face appear kind . . . and familiar.

"Braegon?" said Shaka. Indeed, this man had Rayla's unmistakable hair and eyes, and Maestro's strong jaw.

"How do you know that name?" the man inquired.

"We visited the home of Rayla and Maestro not three days' journey from here," Shaka replied.

"Yes, I am Braegon, and I can see you have much to tell. Pray say that my parents are well, and tell me where I shall find them. I have searched long and far."

Young but grim he appeared in the stream of sunshine that fell upon him . . .

"They are well and ever awaiting your return, though they fear that their home shifts like the paths. How came you to be here where we journey?" asked Shaka.

"I seek the clearing as the syzygy approaches," said Braegon. "I come to discover the magic of the Woods that keeps me from my home."

"Come with us," said Shaka, "for we seek the same clearing. We seek to fulfill the prophecy."

And then Braegon gazed in wonder at Shaka and Laney, for he knew the dangers of the Woods, and he marveled that this syzygy might be the one foretold in the stories of old.

"If you seek to fulfill the prophecy, then I must help," he said. "I shall not be one to turn my back on such a calling."

"Then in return, when the prophecy is fulfilled, I shall go with you to find the house of Maestro and Rayla."

So it was decided. Laney and Shaka welcomed Braegon. They told him everything about their night with Maestro and Rayla, and he wanted to hear it over and over, questioning every detail. "What did mother play on her violin? Is she still as beautiful as her music? What was father painting?" Every question spawned yet another.

Laney couldn't help but think how many questions she would have about her own family if only she could remember.

Tak and Gallia quickly understood that Braegon meant no harm, and after a brief trial period where they kept him under constant scrutiny, they relaxed in his presence.

The company of travelers now headed in the direction that both Shaka and Braegon agreed would take them to the foretold clearing, and even Laney sensed where they needed to go.

As they marched onward, the forest grew thick with trees from the earliest dawn of the West Woods.

"Never have I seen trees such as these," Shaka commented. "They must be as old as the hills and streams. They have the stature of kings."

Indeed, the trunks were as wide as ten trees in Tarzetta, and the canopy reached into the clouds. "The land of the giants," Laney mused.

The travelers journeyed into the ancient growth, and the ground began to rise. Then just before the hill crested, they came to a fallen tree as large as any they had seen standing. Its trunk rested flush with the ground.

"Perchance we could find a way to climb over it, but the dogs cannot," said Shaka. "We must go around or find a place where we can go under. We shall see how tall this tree once stood."

In the dimly lit forest the tree looked like an endless barrier. They hiked for some time, but instead of finding a way around, they came to two more fallen trees that forced them even farther out of their way.

"I do not think these fallen trees are here by chance," Shaka said. "Rayla was right when she said that the West Woods would resist our presence—'tis happening now."

"Many powers run through the West Woods," said Braegon. "I know not what is behind them, but they are no friend to us."

"Should we go back the other way?" asked Laney.

"My instincts tell me that will not help," said Shaka. "We cannot waste time going back and forth. We must go forward."

Tak barked in agreement and nudged Laney. She gave the dog a questioning look.

"Tak is right," said Shaka. "You need to get us past these trees. Use your powers as you did to break the rocks."

"But it's huge!" said Laney.

"'Tis merely wood. Your spirit is strong—call upon it now!"

Shaka and the dogs took several steps back, and Braegon followed their lead.

Laney took a few deep breaths and thought about how the rocks had shattered. She closed her eyes and cleared her mind. Then she raised her stick and brought it down upon the tree trunk before her. With a sound like the crack of a whip, the stick struck the log.

The tree remained unscathed. "That feeling I had yesterday—it's gone." She turned toward Shaka hoping for advice.

"You *must* remember," said Shaka.

Tak looked at Laney and barked a double bark. Laney felt a shiver go down her back. She looked into Tak's eyes and saw not distress, but confidence. She put her hand on the handle of the Blade of Kramariton, and echoes of Tak's bark at the great arch filled her mind. "That's it," she said. She raised her stick once again, and with one smooth sure stroke rained it down upon the fallen tree.

A blinding flash, a deafening boom—a gaping hole appeared, like a tunnel through a mountain.

"Wow!" said Laney when she opened her eyes.

"I had no doubt," said Shaka.

Braegon nodded to Laney. "The prophecy is nigh," he said. "The tale of old comes now before us. Let us go to meet it."

The Clearing

As soon as they passed through to the other side of the fallen tree, the weather changed. Thick flakes of snow fell like cotton. The wind picked up, lifting and swirling the flakes.

Hours seemed to pass, and the snow rose from their toes toward their knees. The dogs struggled.

Then suddenly the trees gave way, and the travelers stumbled into a clearing.

"I've been here before," said Laney. "In a dream or for real, I don't know, but I've been here before."

"Indeed," said Shaka. "You *are* the Sorceress from the West."

The wind gusted, and the low-lying clouds parted, revealing the sun.

"This is where we are meant to be," declared Shaka. "The time is almost upon us." She looked to the sky, and the edge of the sun began to disappear. "The syzygy has begun. Now is the time—our time. The wolves shall come."

"I do not fear the wolves," said Braegon, "though I know not how we will stand against them."

The wind whipped the snow into a frenzy, and they could see no more than a few paces ahead. Shaka and Laney kept close together, and the dogs flanked their sides. Braegon plunged ahead.

"We shall need these no more," said Shaka, removing her pack and motioning for Laney to do the same. Shaka discarded her walking stick as well. She readied her crossbow with a Destiny arrow and sniffed the air. "No wolves yet," she said. "I shall smell them before they are upon us."

Shaka now moved with the caution of a lioness stalking prey, and Laney followed closely with the wind and the snow swirling around them.

Braegon might have been just a few paces away, but he now walked out of sight and earshot. With each step he drifted farther from the others as he followed a familiar sound, one that he sensed rather than heard—his mother's violin. And at the same time, in the same direction, he saw faint glimmers of light, like fireflies hovering in the distance, or perhaps candle flames dancing in the wind.

Shaka and Laney neither heard nor sensed what drew Braegon away, and they continued into the unknown. And then just when Shaka realized that she no longer knew which way she must go, the blinding snow gave way to a gust of winter's breath. The snowflakes parted like fluttering curtains, and a shape appeared—large and gray. It came toward them. Shaka raised her crossbow.

Another gust, and the snow retreated as if it were no more than wisps of smoke, and before them stood a woman of most unusual elegance. Her gown appeared woven of reeds, and her hat sprouted grass and flowers. Two crickets crawled among the greenery.

"You are not real!" Shaka proclaimed. "You are here, yet you are not." The swirling wind and snow resumed, but with no effect on the woman, her flowers, or her crickets.

The woman smiled at Shaka and then turned her gaze to Laney. "You dreamt of me—do you remember?"

Laney hesitated, and then said, "A green violin—do you play a green violin?"

"Yes, you have heard my music in your travels."

Shaka grabbed Laney's arm. "Not all that we see and hear is real," she said.

But Laney was mesmerized by this woman. "Who are you?" she asked.

"I am Chirr, and I have been looking after you, Laney."

"I don't understand," said Laney. "Nothing makes any sense."

"It does not matter that you do not understand," replied Chirr. "If you know what you must do, then understand or not, you must do it."

"I don't understand," said Laney. "Nothing makes any sense."

"Where are the wolves and the black fog?" asked Laney.

"They will come," said Chirr.

Shaka stepped in front of Laney. "Then you will help us," she said to Chirr.

Chirr continued to smile. "How can I help you if I am not real?"

"Forgive my manners," said Shaka. "Help us, and I will know you are real."

"I am as real as you are—are you real?" Chirr challenged without losing her smile.

"Help us or be gone," Shaka snapped. "I am not here to answer riddles."

"But maybe I am," Laney said, locking eyes with Chirr.

"You wear the Sun Stone," said Chirr. "Let its power guide you. Am I friend or foe?"

"You are . . . a friend," said Laney.

"Good. Now what do you see over here?" Chirr turned and pointed.

Laney took a few steps in that direction, unable to see more than a short ways in front of her as the snow continued to swirl. Meanwhile, Shaka turned in the other direction. A scowl spread across her face. "Do you smell them?" she bellowed. "The wolves are near!" She raised her crossbow fitted with the azure arrow of Destiny.

Now Laney and Shaka were separated and neither could see anything but snow. The dogs barked from what seemed like far away. If Chirr remained, Laney could no longer see her.

Laney continued to walk forward, drawn by an urge she did not understand but did not wish to deny. A step, and then another and another. Out of the swirls of blinding white, a wall appeared—a building with brown bricks, and a window. She stepped to the window and peered inside. Children in a classroom—kindergarten. One child caught her attention, though his back was toward her. The child turned.

"Laney, what are you doing here?" he asked, his voice muffled but distinct through the pane of glass.

"Ryan!"

"Laney, what are you doing here?"

From what seemed like miles away, or perhaps worlds away, Laney heard Shaka's desperate warning, "The wolves are coming! The wolves!"

Laney turned to the sound of Shaka's voice and, without a thought of what she might do to help, raced toward the wolves.

Then, as if the West Woods were taunting them, the sky cleared, and the sickly cast of eclipsed sunlight revealed in the distance the sea of wolves stretching as far as any eyes could see. And seemingly from nowhere, wisps of black mist swirled at Laney's feet and all around, and then thicker and higher it rose, and with it came an abominable stench.

The black fog had arrived.

"Tak, Gallia, stay!" Shaka commanded.

Shaka and the dogs held their ground—but Laney raced toward the wolves.

Shaka stared in disbelief. She unleashed arrow after arrow to rain down upon the wolves. But arrows of a thousand archers would have made no difference.

Out of breath and alone before the wolves, Laney stopped. In a moment the beasts would be upon her, lunging for her throat. Laney raised her staff and yelled, "I remember!" and thrust it into the earth. At once with a roar like thunder, the staff shattered and the ground cracked and fell apart before her, opening into a chasm that stretched to either side as far as the eye could see. The earth's gaping wound swallowed up scores of wolves, while others stopped short, howling in frustration.

Braegon continued to follow the music and the lights. Illusion or not, he knew he had to respond. "I hear you!" he said, and his words spanned the gap between dreams and reality such that Rayla, asleep in her bed, smiled and knew that somehow she and Braegon had found each other. Braegon raced deep into the clearing, heeding not the smell of the wolves until the stench almost stifled his breath. Then he fitted an arrow in his great bow and called out, "I am coming!" though he knew not whether he called to his mother or the wolves. But at that moment the power of the Sorceress of the West coursed through the earth, ripping it apart almost at his feet. He fell to the ground before the crevasse that stretched its cavernous void beyond sight, and on all fours he scrambled to avoid the crumbling edge. The roar of the splitting earth drowned out all other sounds.

Braegon scrambled to his feet and watched as his vision of lights disappeared into the black fog—while far, far away, he and the clearing vanished from Rayla's dream.

Though the vast army of wolves stood stranded on the far side of the crevasse, some in the vanguard had gotten through, and they resumed their charge. But now the fight was fair, and Shaka was ready. The first wolf leapt for Shaka, but she was too quick, and an arrow of Destiny pierced its throat. The wolf fell dead at her feet. Seconds later another charged, and again a Destiny arrow found its mark. Three more wolves held their distance from Shaka, but others charged toward Laney. Shaka saw them coming and yelled, "Laney, look out!" She fired a golden arrow of Protection, and then another, as fast as her hands could move. Two wolves lay dead.

Tak and Gallia barked a warning—a giant of a wolf bounded toward Shaka. Gallia leaped forward and met the wolf head-on, but the wolf tossed her like a rabbit. Shaka yelled in rage as she fitted another arrow. The wolf charged as if driven by a blind fury. Shaka let loose the arrow of Wrath, and its point drilled into the wolf up to the violet threads in the arrow's shaft—but the wolf kept coming. Shaka reached into her quiver and grabbed another arrow, willing her hands to move lightning quick to ready her crossbow. But the festering wound in her arm had taken its toll, and in spite of her indomitable will, her hands betrayed her—before she could fit the arrow, the wolf pounced.

Shaka and the wolf crashed to the ground, and the arrow flew from Shaka's hand as if shot into the air. It landed harmlessly, buried in the snow up to its black feathers. The force of the wolf upon Shaka snapped her crossbow, sending shards of wood flying into the air.

Laney watched the attack upon Shaka, and time seemed to slow. Details magnified. Splinters of Shaka's crossbow floated through the air; Tak leaped, momentarily suspended in air, and barred his teeth, ready to tear into Shaka's wolf.

And then Laney felt a chill behind her, greater than any cold of ice and snow, and she turned. There before her, not twenty paces away, stood a beast unlike any Earthly creature—black as pitch, tall as a horse, winged like a bat. Slobber dripped from between its ragged teeth as it snarled and advanced, its smoldering eyes locked on Laney.

A stench of pure evil washed over Laney, and she felt faint. Her hand fell upon the handle of her knife, the Blade of Kramariton. She drew it from its sheath. And as the blade revealed itself, so too did Laney's courage. She held the blade aloft and let out a battle cry the likes of which had never before been heard in the clearing. She stepped toward the beast.

The beast stopped and snarled, for no longer did it see prey. A blade of old and a warrior with the stature to wield it—never had the beast encountered any such challenge. The beast stepped back.

But two wolves charged from the side, and Laney, her will bent upon the beast, failed to see. The first wolf leaped.

Out of the corner of her eye she finally saw the threat, and with a speed that even Shaka could not have matched, Laney turned and swung the Blade of Kramariton. And though she had no skills with a knife, the blade nonetheless found its mark upon the outstretched neck of the wolf—such was the power of this blade and the one who wielded it. Then the second wolf leaped. Laney thrust the Blade of Kramariton with such force that when it struck the chest of the wolf, the blade all but disappeared—but the wolf landed upon Laney, and both fell to the ground.

. . . the great beast bounded forward . . .

Laney winced in pain as she yanked her arm from beneath the body of the wolf. But when her hand came free, it no longer held the Blade of Kramariton. And before she could act to retrieve it, she faced another threat. The first wolf, gravely wounded, snorted and bared its teeth, so close now that Laney could smell its foul breath. She jumped to her feet and backed away, her eyes fixed upon the wolf. The wolf wobbled forward, snarled, and readied itself for a final lunge. But the glint in its eyes turned dark, and it fell and hissed its last breath.

Now Laney might retrieve the Blade of Kramariton—but the great beast bounded forward and stood upon the carcass where the blade lay buried.

The beast beat its wings, and the black fog billowed all around, for the beast and the fog were one, made whole by the magical syzygy.

The beast tore apart the carcass upon which it stood, and then the beast came for Laney.

She backed away a step, and another and another. And as she retreated, so too did the hope of the prophecy. The beast now opened its massive jaws and flared its nostrils, savoring the inevitable. Laney took one final step back, halted by a jolt from behind—the window to Ryan's classroom! Laney's head bounced off the pane with a dull thud.

The beast stopped just five paces away. With her back and head pressed against the schoolhouse window, Laney could hear children inside talking and laughing. Only she and a pane of glass stood between their cheery innocence and the jaws of the beast. And with that realization, there stirred in Laney a strength she had never known.

"Not today!" she yelled, each word seeming to last an eternity. She looked up at the sky, and now the moon had reached its peak in the eclipse. The syzygy had come, and now it would go. A wand, a stick, something to channel her energy—Laney looked to either side—nothing—but then she saw the feathers of Shaka's arrow, now right beside her. She thrust her hand into the snow and grabbed the shaft. As she pulled it from the snow, the beast bounded toward her and leaped.

The body of the beast descended upon her, and so too did a vision from Laney's dreams: a black raptor plummeting with impossible speed—and Laney knew it to be Death. In an instant the dream and the beast became one—claws and talons, teeth and beak, a mass of darkness. But unlike the dream, Laney now wielded a weapon, and though it was but a single arrow, it gave her hope beyond measure. She thrust the arrow with all her might, burying the point in the beast's chest with such force that it penetrated up to her clenched fist. The beast was upon her, and the blow of its body sent them both crashing through the window. Glass showered the classroom as Laney and the beast slammed into the floor. The arrow still clenched in Laney's unyielding fist snapped from the force of their landing. Darkness descended upon her mind, and she knew this world no more.

The broken arrow tumbled from Laney's limp hand, clattering onto the floor, its shaft adorned with the crimson thread of Sacrifice.

And yet the prophecy was fulfilled, for in that moment the beast released its last gurgling breath, and the fire in its eyes disappeared. The wind changed direction and a gust the strength of a gale blew from the east, carrying away the black fog and stench that had accompanied the beast. And as the moon danced past the sun, ushering in a new dawn, light shone upon the West Woods with such brilliance that the snow sparkled as if it were diamonds, and the trees seemed to stretch their limbs as if awakening to the coming of spring. The evil hold upon the West Woods was broken, and the wolves looked about wondering why they had gathered, as if they had just awoken to the vanishing of a bad dream. They scattered into small packs and, most being on the far side of the chasm, headed back toward the Northwest Mountains.

Shaka stirred under a dead wolf, her violet arrow having finally completed its task, and Tak helped pull the animal aside. Shaka got to her knees, and Gallia came to her side, bloodied but able. Shaka pulled herself to her feet and half stumbled, half ran.

"Laney!" Shaka cried, but she was too late.

Back Again

From the emptiness of oblivion came an unlikely sound—the vibrato of a classical violin. Penetrating the darkness, traveling the unimaginable distance between here, the hereafter, and back to the middle of Linden Road, the sound arrived at its final destination crisp and clear. After days in a distant world but seconds in ours, the vibration of the four strings reached not only Laney's ears but also her brain. Vivaldi's *The Four Seasons – "Winter"* blasted from the car radio, oblivious to the destruction surrounding it—the collapsed steering wheel, the disheveled dash belching impotent airbags, the crystals of windshield glass littering the road, and the hood of the car replaced by the trunk of the largest oak in town. Acorns rolled from the roof of the car as leaves settled in their place. Laney's notebook and a museum brochure featuring the Michael Cheval exhibit lay in the snow beyond the tree.

Laney's fingers twitched—an involuntary movement, her first sign of life. A shrill ". . . My God! Laney! LANEY!" interrupted the music—her mother screaming. Laney opened her eyes amidst the disarray.

A good Samaritan pried open Laney's driver-side door and said something about calling 911, but Laney paid him no mind. The tails of a dream fled from her as awareness of the moment took hold, and she found herself saying "arrow" without any notion as to why. She looked at her mother sitting beside her, but there were no answers there—just panic that only a mother can know. And now more faces looked into Laney's open door.

"Is anyone hurt?" an onlooker asked.

"What happened?" Laney asked, to no one in particular.

"You swerved right into this tree," a woman offered.

"I saw it," another woman said. "A squirrel ran out, and you tried to stop."

A squirrel—now Laney remembered. It had darted in front of the car and then stopped like a deer in headlights. It had looked right at her as she jammed the brakes and jerked the wheel. She remembered the screech of the tires, like the shriek of a giant bird. The car jumping the curb. The massive oak with outstretched limbs—a murder of crows fleeing the branches as the car targeted the tree. The sudden realization of the inevitable, when all choices disappeared and the accident became as definite and immutable as if it had already happened.

Laney rubbed her neck and rolled her head from side to side. Everything hurt, but she was okay.

Mother and daughter both got out of the car and sat down in the snow. They looked over at the smashed car, and without saying a word they both knew how lucky they were.

A police car arrived some minutes later, the whining of the siren drowning out Laney's thoughts. Then the fire and rescue vehicle joined the chorus of noise—sirens and shouting, with the car radio providing a surreal accompaniment of classical music.

Laney and her mother both insisted they were fine and rebuffed the forceful recommendations that they be taken to the hospital. The police took a full report, called a towing company, and then drove Laney and her mother the short distance to their home.

Laney stayed home that night. She was grounded, and even if she weren't, she had no energy. She went to her bedroom early, wondering as she climbed the stairs what additional punishments might arrive with the next day.

She sat on her bed, facing the window, and listened to the wind rattle the panes. The sound reminded her of one of the neighborhood boys, Jason, tossing

"A squirrel ran out, and you tried to stop."

pebbles at her window when they both should have been sleeping. She liked the attention more than she liked Jason.

She came to the window and peered into the darkness. She put her hand upon the pane, felt it shiver with each gust, and imagined the force of the wind blowing through the trees, bending even the greatest boughs, stripping their leaves. And as the vibrations from the window went from her fingertips to her mind, she felt an overpowering sense that she belonged out there standing on the forest floor, smelling the scent of pine swirling in the crisp night air. She opened her window, and the blast of northern air sent a chill through her, a tantalizing tingle. She felt déjà vu—from her childhood? No—something more present. She turned out the lights and returned to the open window. She leaned out into the night air, savoring the surrounding darkness and breeze upon her face and shoulders, allowing the sensation to bring her closer to the magic that she felt. And in that instant, as if she had somehow traveled to a distant time and place, Laney envisioned herself in an endless forest, on a path—a dirt trail with patches of snow. Laney's mind traveled deeper along the path, and the weight of her imagination threatened to tip her precariously. And then the bark of a dog interrupted the melody of the wind, a bark so close she fancied she could smell the dog. And then a double bark. "Tak!" she said, and now standing erect once again she reached to touch the dog beside her. Her hand sank into the warm thick fur, and she looked down as the dog nudged her leg.

"Major, it's you," she said as the magic of the wind disappeared. The faithful family dog looked inquisitively at her. "What was I saying?" she asked the German shepherd, but Major made no reply.

Laney closed the window and turned the lights back on, and then sat on the bed looking at Major, who had come to sit obediently at her feet.

"That was weird," she said, and stood to get ready for bed. She needed a good night's sleep like never before. She started to change into her nightclothes, and that's when she felt something under her shirt. She struggled to lift the collar over her head and pull her arms out, and when the shirt finally came off, it revealed a necklace. She looked at the orange-red stone entwined in an almost white silvery metal, and wondered how on Earth she had come to be wearing it. Was it new, something she had gotten that day and then forgotten because of the accident? She backtracked in her mind to the start of the day, an ordinary day—granola cereal with extra spoonfuls of sugar when her mom wasn't looking—Ryan spilling a glass of milk—or was that the day before? Her father hurrying out the door—could have been any day. Then the art museum for her school paper. Had she gone to the gift shop and purchased anything? She didn't remember doing that. She recalled that when her mom and Ryan left the museum, she had looked at the strange paintings, and then she had briefly fallen asleep on one of the benches—museums had that effect. She'd awakened in time to call her mom to come get her, and from there she practiced her driving. She remembered the day—most of it anyway—up to the moment of the accident. But not the necklace. She held it up to the light and watched it sparkle—she liked it.

She said goodnight to Major, and put the necklace on the nightstand and her head on the pillow. But thoughts of her day kept racing around in her head. She couldn't help but feel that something wasn't quite right—but what? Was there something she needed to do?

She had no answers. She closed her eyes and thought, *I'll figure it out tomorrow.*

The School

Laney awoke to the start of what felt like just another day. When she got dressed, she put on the necklace, but then as she looked at herself in the mirror, she tucked it inside her shirt. She came downstairs almost tiptoeing, wondering whether her parents would be angry after fully digesting the fact that she had totaled their second car. But luckily for Laney, her dad was in a hurry, as usual, rushing about, a coffee cup in one hand, briefcase in another, and probably wishing he had a third hand to collect his phone, keys, and everything else he might need before heading out the door. And her mom was engrossed in the daily crossword puzzle, a pen pressed against her lips as if restraining them from opening and begging for help.

"What's an eight-letter word for 'home'?" she finally blurted out in frustration.

"Domicile," Laney's dad replied without missing a beat.

"Okay, one more. I need a six-letter word for 'planetary alignment.'"

"Eclipse," he replied again.

"No, that's seven letters—I need six."

"Syzygy," Laney said without thinking.

Her father choked on his coffee, spilling some onto his briefcase. He set the dripping cup down on the counter and turned to Laney. "What?" he said.

"S-Y-Z-Y-G-Y. It fits," said Laney's mom, and she gave that "Who are you?" look reserved for times when Laney's behavior defied explanation. But Laney just shrugged her shoulders and turned her back to stuff a waffle into the toaster. *Why did I say anything?* she thought, and then, *What did I just say?*

But a moment later her father was out the door, and her mother was preoccupied filling in the last few words to complete her puzzle.

Laney grabbed the waffle as it popped out of the toaster, slung her backpack over her shoulder, and headed out to her bus stop. "Bye, Laney!" said Ryan, and Laney gave him a rare smile as she stepped out the door.

She felt relieved as soon as the door closed behind her, as if gravity had less force in the fresh air. The day was starting out okay, she thought, as she arrived at the corner to the sound of squeaky brakes grinding the school bus to a halt. She stepped inside, where the inescapable exhaust fumes and bouncy ride would provide a lingering nausea to accompany the start of her first class.

Laney, as always, wrinkled her nose as if to adjust it to the smell, and then she found an empty seat and scooted to the window. She liked that snug feeling of leaning against the side of the bus, and she liked to feel the sun shining on her face. As she sat there, she reached to scratch an itch—*Why do shirts have tags on the collar?* she thought, and her hand touched the necklace. She pulled it out to have another look. In the bright sunlight the stone shimmered a rainbow of colors, but at the same time seemed to have an unexpected depth, as if the center of the stone were drawing her gaze inward. She moved the stone closer to her eyes, and the interplay of the light among the translucent layers had an almost hypnotic effect. She let her mind drift, and again, as she had experienced the previous night, she found herself thinking about a forest—not just thinking about it—experiencing it. Snow filtered through the trees and settled in patches along a path that wound its way into the distance.

"Come on!" Laney felt a hand on her shoulder and heard the familiar voice of her classmate, Mandy. The image of the forest disappeared.

Laney liked her biology class because Mr. Wiggins believed that science should not be confined to the classroom. He took the students on walks to identify aspens and alders, spruce and pines. He pointed to bees' nests and raccoons' dens and so many other things they otherwise wouldn't notice. He always knew where to poke a stick to find bugs and snakes. The class didn't get to go outside every day, but more often than not, at least once a week, they would head out into the elements to explore and discover. And today was one of those days. Mr. Wiggins beamed like a child with a birthday cake as he waited impatiently for his young scientists to take their seats. He came around to the front of his desk to get closer to the class to share the good news: today they would see a solar eclipse. He had set up a telescope with an approved solar filter, and he had made makeshift eclipse-viewing devices out of cardboard and paper. In addition, he had procured enough eclipse sunglasses for the whole class. After a few opening remarks, during which he could hardly contain his excitement, Mr. Wiggins, with his arms full of boxes and papers, led the class outside to Phil Field, the grassy area between the school and the woods.

"It's already started," he said, brimming with delight. Then, "No!—don't look at it without your glasses!"

Mandy giggled as Mr. Wiggins fussed over the eclipse, and Laney would have been laughing too except that something was making her restless, nagging at her with greater persistence each passing hour. There was something she wanted to remember, but what?

Finally she put on her eclipse glasses and looked up at the sky. *Looks like mud*, she thought. But as she tilted her head back and the start of the eclipse came into view, an overwhelming déjà vu hit her like an exploding airbag. And in that instant, she remembered.

"What the . . ." Her words trailed off as memories from the West Woods came flooding back. Shaka, Tak, and Gallia—how could she have forgotten them and their quest? The West Woods—a dream? No, something more. The memory felt as real as any she possessed, more vivid and coherent than any dream, so real the experience had, at the time, eclipsed all other reality, blotting out not only everything she now knew to be real but also all memory of her former self. She felt her face flush, as if she had just been awakened from a hypnotic trance to find herself standing on a stage with an audience clapping and her not understanding where she was or why.

What did it mean?—the art museum, the Michael Cheval exhibit, the painting of the huntress—Shaka. Could Shaka be real? What had happened that afternoon when Laney left the exhibit hall? Had she wandered in the wilderness to Shaka's home, or had she napped and then gone for a driving lesson with her mother? Both seemed real.

And then she heard Ogmo's words in her head as clearly as if he were standing before her: *A squirrel will change your life—it has already happened!* The squirrel . . . the accident . . . the West Woods, Shaka, Ogmo, Chirr, the beast . . . Ryan. Ryan—he was there and here! He had awakened the whole house with a nightmare the night before her accident. *"It's real—the monster's coming! Laney, you were there—tell Mommy you're going to fight the monster,"* he had said. Ryan had drawn the picture that Shaka found in Laney's backpack. In the clearing, he had been there, in the school when the monster came. Somehow her adventure was about him. The brother who loved gummy bears and drew her silly pictures. Was he in danger? The school, the syzygy—Ryan was there then and now.

The old Laney would have shrugged off any number of coincidences and embraced her cloak of indifference—but the old Laney was gone. In the blink of an eye that spanned eleven long days, she had changed.

I must get to him, she thought, *and make sure he's safe. No time to explain to anyone—no one would understand.*

His school was less than a mile away. She could get there.

"It doesn't matter that you don't understand," she said aloud, remembering the words of Chirr.

Mandy chuckled. "How shall we ever thank Mr. Wiggins?" she said, thinking Laney's words were mocking their teacher.

Laney took off the dark glasses and put her hand to her chest, feeling the necklace from her dreams. She reached beneath her collar and pulled out the crystal—it was real. Her dream was real.

She began to back away toward the trees, and after a few steps, turned and ran. Mandy stifled a laugh but did not follow.

Laney moved through the maze of evergreens and birches with ease. She had played among those trees ever since she was a child, and she knew the woods to be a shortcut across town.

She popped out of the woods at the top of a hill overlooking the neighborhood leading to Ryan's school. With the wind at her back, she sailed down the hill as fast as her legs would allow.

Her head felt clear, more so than ever before, as if she were truly awake for the first time. She headed directly where she needed to go, cutting through yards, leaping over a picket fence and scaling a chain link fence, charging past barking dogs. One more street plus two back-to-back yards, and Ryan's school came into view—an old brick building reminiscent of a factory long past its prime. From kindergarten through fifth grade, all the classrooms were filled.

Ryan and his classmates all worked their scissors on orange and black construction paper. Some children cut out pumpkins and scary-looking jack-o'-lanterns, while others tried their best to make bats without clipping their wings. Scraps of paper and globs of paste littered the tables and floor.

"Ryan, what is this we're making?" asked Mrs. Whitfield.

"It's a monster," said Ryan, and he held up the paper, shaking it to show that it was indeed ferocious.

"Well, that looks super scary," said Mrs. Whitfield as she raised her hands in feigned panic.

"I'm not afraid," said Ryan.

A car pulled into the school parking lot, a gray, boxy vehicle with spots of rust. The engine turned off, car door opened, and a clean-cut man stepped onto the blacktop. His trench coat suited the unseasonably cold day, but he wore it for reasons other than warmth. With his right hand, he held a cigarette to his lips, but his left hand lay beneath the front of his coat, gripping the handle of his concealed weapon of choice, an Uzi. With a hint of a smile he took note of the peaceful, almost idyllic, setting. He would change that.

Why Ryan's school? No one can say, for it is the nature of evil that "Why?" is never answered in a satisfactory manner. Evil defies logic and reason—it is an anomaly of the human condition, a mutation of the soul. In our dreams evil takes the shape of monsters, hideous to behold, but in the waking world it often has a pleasant smile.

The man finished his cigarette and flicked it away. A shadow grew upon the land as if a dark cloud had formed overhead—the eclipse had begun. A gust of wind blew open the man's trench coat revealing his weapon, but secrecy no longer mattered. He headed toward the school building, a spring in his step.

When Laney saw the man's car pull into the school lot, a chill ran down her spine. She was already at the lot when the car stopped, and halfway across it when she heard the car door slam shut. When she reached the front doors of the school, she looked back and saw the man, his coat open and flapping in the wind, his hand on the weapon. She flung open the door and rushed inside.

She ran down the hall. A fire alarm—she pulled the lever. The alarm blared through the corridors.

The principal and her assistant stepped outside the administrative office—they had not scheduled a drill. Laney rounded the corner and almost ran into them.

"There's a man with a gun!" Laney yelled as loud as she could. "Get everyone down, away from windows! Call the police! Now, do it NOW!"

The principal and her assistant exchanged confused glances and then looked in both directions at the empty hallway. The alarm, a surreal interruption to the meticulously planned school day, could not be ignored. "Did you pull the fire alarm?" the principal said, more a reprimand than a question.

"Yes, it's not a fire—call the police!"

"Come with me." The principal grabbed Laney's arm and led her into her office. With the flick of a switch, the school intercom turned on.

"Intruder alert!" the principal announced. "This is not a drill. Everyone move away from the windows and lie down on the floor. Teachers, close your classroom doors, and block them shut until you receive further instructions. There is no fire—this is an intruder alert."

Then she dialed 911.

The principal hung up the phone. "Young lady, if this is a prank you're in a lot of trouble," she scolded. "Wait right here until the police arrive."

Almost on cue they heard a pop-pop-pop-pop-pop immediately followed by the sound of glass shattering onto a hard floor—it came from the front of the building. A moment later, more popping and crashing glass.

Laney bolted from the administrative office. The principal's assistant grabbed her arm, but Laney broke free. She raced toward Ryan's classroom, the kindergarten room at the far west side of the building. As she ran, the popping and jangle of shattered glass followed her down the hall.

Almost there. Time seemed to slow, and her senses sharpened. She became acutely aware of every instant and detail—the booming of her heart, the rasping of her lungs, the approaching door.

The doorknob turned in her hand, and she burst into the room.

The teacher, Mrs. Whitfield, froze, or so it appeared to Laney as each instant grew in magnitude. The children lay on the floor, face-down. Including Ryan.

The bullets came in quick succession, whizzing past Laney and through the far wall. As the glass fell, the shooter moved into view. And being at the end of the building with no more windows to shoot, he jumped through the gaping window into the middle of the classroom. He sneered as he turned his gaze toward Laney.

. . . he turned his gaze toward Laney.

But today was the day of the syzygy presiding over dreams and reality—a day of opportunity. The school, Ryan, the monster, and Laney—a new Laney tempered by her trials in the West Woods—had converged in the shadow of the moon. And as she had faced the monster in the West Woods, so too did Laney at this final moment stand her ground. Absent her staff and the crimson arrow, her hands fell upon Mrs. Whitfield's red golf umbrella resting in its usual place beside the door. She seized it with both hands and charged.

The shooter swung his Uzi toward her. His finger squeezed the trigger—shots spewed across the room. The umbrella jerked—a bullet passed through, red threads flying. Another, coming at Laney's head—the moment amplified a thousandfold. The bullet nipped her scalp.

Then, before another shot fired, Laney thrust the red umbrella.

The unlikely weapon hit with such force that the shaft broke in her hands. The point sank deep into the shooter's chest.

With a look of disbelief, the shooter collapsed. The malevolent glint in his eyes vanished, and the Uzi fell to the floor. Laney kicked it aside.

"Children, line up, quickly!" Mrs. Whitfield shouted, and for the first time that anyone could remember, she wasn't talking down to them.

Through the shattered window, the outside chill gusted into Laney's face as she stood over the shooter. For a moment she felt as if she were in both worlds at once, that the breeze in her face carried the scent of pine from the West Woods.

She looked up, through the window's western view, as the sun and the moon now began moving apart. Then she felt something on her hand—Ryan slipping his little fingers into her palm. "Laney, let's go," he said as he tugged at her.

She squeezed his hand. "You knew I'd come, didn't you?"

"Yeah, always," said Ryan.

Laney shook her head. "Not always," she said, "but from now on."

She walked Ryan toward the far wall where most of the children stood crying. Then she helped some of the children who were too frightened to move, talking calmly to them and holding their hands as they joined the others. Mrs. Whitfield opened the door and stuck her head out into the hallway. Fire alarms rang through the corridors, but the halls remained empty. The threat had passed.

Within a matter of minutes more police cars, fire engines, and ambulances converged on the school than anyone had ever seen. Even the old-timers had no stories to match. Soon choppers from the local news circled overhead. News vans pulled up to the rescue vehicles, and reporters and cameramen pushed their way as far forward as the police would allow.

The police entered the building in full riot gear with shields ready and weapons drawn.

Curious and concerned onlookers gathered quickly as word spread at the speed of cell phones.

"Sergeant Cruise!" one of the reporters yelled over the din of the crowd and sirens. She shoved a microphone toward the officer. "Tell our viewers what's happening."

But Sergeant Cruise was busy taping off the area to control the growing crowd. "Not now!" he barked.

The reporter turned to another policeman and put her hand on his arm to get his attention. "Officer, what can you tell us? Have any children been hurt?"

"We have officers in the building, and when we know more, we'll let you know. Now get back," he ordered. "This is a restricted area."

Minutes later, two of the officers who had entered the school came back out with their guns holstered. "All clear," said one of them to his captain. "One shooter down. Paramedics just gave up on him. No other casualties."

"Who got him?" asked the captain, a woman with wrinkles beyond her years.

"A civilian, ma'am, a high-school girl with an umbrella. Stabbed him in the chest. Stabbed him so hard the umbrella broke in half. Amazing what adrenaline can do."

"A girl with an umbrella—and on a sunny day, no less. I want to talk with her."

When the police questioned Laney, there were some raised eyebrows but no reprimand for skipping class in the middle of the school day. The officers didn't know what to make of her explanation that she went to Ryan's school because of a bad dream, but they could find no other mischief to account for her behavior, so they let the matter rest. Laney was a hero. She had singlehandedly prevented the worst disaster in the town's history, and as far as the authorities were concerned, that was the end of the story. The police took the broken umbrella into evidence to be filed away until the end of time, and the paramedics carted off the body of the shooter for investigation and identification.

The school closed the next day, but repairs happened quickly. The building reopened the following week, staffed with extra counselors to help children overcome their fears. But the resilience of the young often surprises grownups, even the experts, and soon the tenor of the classrooms returned to normal. Even Laney, whom the authorities felt needed special attention, quickly transitioned back to her typical school routine, the impact of taking a life overshadowed by those she had saved. In fact, the events that Laney replayed over and over in her head were not those of the school shooting but rather her journey through the West Woods.

After the attack on the school, some teachers had a difficult time adjusting—Mrs. Whitfield in particular. For weeks she went without an umbrella, even on rainy days, and at times she seemed to have lost her kindergarten voice. But finally a Monday came with Mrs. Whitfield clicking the point of a new umbrella on the hallway floor, and to everyone's surprise it was as green as a leprechaun's hat. "It's the other Christmas color," she said.

The Exhibit

A few weeks after that fateful day at the school, Laney asked to go back to the art museum. Her term paper needed work, but the real reason for the visit was to take another look at the Michael Cheval exhibit. She wanted to see whether some magic still lingered at those paintings.

"Your mother will need to come get you," her father said as they pulled in front of the museum. "She won't have the car until lunchtime, but call her then."

"Okay," said Laney.

She waved goodbye and headed up the steps to the museum's front doors. Once inside, she headed straight to the Michael Cheval exhibit.

On her way down the main corridor, she saw a man in a security-guard uniform standing outside the impressionist galleries. "Excuse me," she said. "Are the exits in the gallery rooms alarmed?" Not that an alarm would deter her. She wanted to see what lay on the other side of the exit door beside *Love Hunter II*, and for her, curiosity often proved to be a powerful force.

"Missy, we don't have emergency exits inside gallery rooms. We don't want people exiting with our paintings. All the exits are in the main hallways, plus the stairwells, and of course the main entrance. But you should use the front entrance like everybody else and leave the other doors alone."

Laney turned without saying a word and headed toward the Michael Cheval exhibit—down the hall, around a corner, past the banner, and up to the exhibit hall door. But the door beneath the ornate arch was closed, and the sign on it read "Closed." She tested the handle, but the door was indeed locked.

"There's a leak in the ceiling." A young woman approached to talk with Laney. No doubt she worked for the museum. "I think they'll reopen soon, if you don't mind waiting," she said.

Drip, drip, drip, Laney thought. *Life imitating . . . dreams?* One way or another, she would get back inside that exhibit. She thanked the woman. Then she sat down right there with her back against the wall. She fished her cell phone out of her backpack and turned her attention to texting.

Soon the exhibit hall door opened, and two men came out carrying a ladder that was so long they almost had to shout to talk as they each carried an end. A moment later a third worker exited the room, pushing a wheeled bucket with his mop. He stopped to remove the "Closed" sign, and water sloshed up to the rim as he started up again, steering the bucket down the hall.

Laney walked through the door and into the midst of the Cheval exhibit. She felt a rush, as if encountering an unexpected friend. These paintings—had they guided her dreams, or were they glimpses of another world? Did Michael Cheval paint from his imagination, or had he somehow experienced the world where Laney journeyed?

Once again the paintings seemed so impossibly real that she half expected them to flow from the boundaries of their frames onto the walls and floors. These creations were more than mere musings of an inspired artist. Somehow they reached beyond the imagination.

Her heart beat faster, and her senses sharpened. Whispers echoed. Dust specks swirled and danced in the spotlights. The smell of perfume—that woman in the purple overcoat who had just entered the room—assaulted Laney's nose with such ferocity that she could taste it as well.

The woman in purple headed into the next hall, and Laney breathed a sigh of relief. She stepped toward the nearest Cheval painting, one she had seen before —*The Muse*. As she had done on her first visit, she followed the flow of the painting's water pipes, but the leak in the ceiling had been fixed, and this time she heard no drip-drip-drip. This painting at least remained confined to its frame, flat and dry in spite of its almost-real imagery.

She turned to the portrait of Zelfore—and then she looked up. A clock did indeed loom above the artwork, a rather loud clock. But each resolute tick of the second hand lasted no longer than the one before—or so it seemed. She looked back at the pendulum clock in Zelfore's hat, and she remembered Maestro telling her that the consistency of time is an illusion. And as she thought that thought, she fancied the clock began to pulse, as if marking time in its imaginary world. But then she realized the pulsing was nothing more than the beating of her heart.

She turned and scanned the room, remembering one painting after another, knowing them as something more than mere fantasy. She recognized Xinni—such beautiful blue hair—and Ogmo, silently behind her. And farther down stood Maestro, painting with his inspiration, the ever-radiant Rayla.

Laney now cast her gaze toward the painting she most wanted to see, that of Shaka. *Love Hunter II*. She hurried toward it, seeking confirmation that what she had experienced was real. She stopped squarely in front of the artwork and gazed into the eyes of the painted figure, close enough to cast her halting breath upon the varnished surface. And Laney in that very moment sensed undeniable history. This was a woman that she had known—her friend, her companion, her mentor—the woman who had made her believe in herself, and believe that anything is possible if you don't give up.

Laney looked into the eyes of the painted Shaka, probing for a connection. But these painted eyes appeared as nothing more than that, and if a soul lay beneath the painted glint, Laney could not discern it. She broke her stare and looked at the floor below the painting—no arrow.

A museum guard stood at the far corner of the room, and Laney approached him to inquire about whether any of the paintings had props.

"I'm security, young lady," he said. "I'm not sure what they're supposed to have, but I haven't seen anything except the paintings. They might be able to help you at the reception area where you first came in."

She thanked him and headed back to the paintings. She stopped in front of *Midsummer Chirr.* Chirr appeared even more alive in the painting than what Laney remembered from the clearing. The visiting cricket was gone, and only the painted one remained.

She stepped to *Stairway to Heaven*, the painting with the young woman who looked like her. But this time the girl seemed different—not remarkably different, but subtly so, such that she would no longer mistake it as a portrait of herself.

She reached for her cell phone and checked the time—a few minutes after noon. Her mom should have the car by now, but Laney wasn't ready to leave. She sat for a moment on a bench in the middle of the room, the same bench she remembered from her previous visit. She had difficulty separating her dream world from her life before and after—had she actually sat on this very bench, or was that the beginning of her dream? So many thoughts raced through her mind—she couldn't keep up with them. Her adventure in the West Woods played back as if every day there were happening at once, and at the same time she couldn't help thinking about the accident. The instant the car jumped the curb, everything happening so fast, and yet with such clarity it appeared as a series of still shots in her brain—bits and pieces maybe missing in between, but certain shots so vivid that every detail became magnified. That collision had threatened to close the book on Laney and set the definition of her life, removing all opportunities for her to alter her place in the world—this world or any other.

But rather than close the book, this collision opened a new chapter—the West Woods. There she had learned to face her fears and to believe that she could do almost anything if she set her mind to it. And she learned that there can be no greater risk than missing the opportunity to protect someone you hold dear.

She heaved a big sigh and headed toward the door. She left the gallery hall, feeling a sense of loss, as if she were abandoning a friend. She couldn't quite bring herself to leave the museum just yet, so instead of calling for a ride, she wandered in the opposite direction from where she had come.

Down that hallway, just before the next corner, the gallery door to the right stood open, and without really looking she somehow realized that this room was also part of the Michael Cheval exhibit. She was already one step past the door when she stopped, turned around, and went inside to have a look.

More than a dozen paintings lined the walls, as vivid and striking as any she had seen before, as realistic and simultaneously impossible as any she could imagine. Nothing she saw at first reminded her of the West Woods adventure, but she felt the paintings somehow were rooted in another time and place. She imagined a story for each one, or were the paintings telling her their stories? Adventure, love, sorrow, and most of all, journeys to strange lands. Worlds underwater, cubed skies, and . . . *Firefly 2*, a painting of an imp inspecting a fruit that looked like Earth. She stepped closer, and then did a double take. The imp looked just like Ryan!

She caught her breath and looked again, and this time the face looked like any child, or none in particular. Her imagination was getting the better of her. She moved on to the next painting, and then the one after that, until she came to one that seemed to jump out at her as she stepped in front of it. A painted squirrel nibbling a nut, with an eye toward Laney, sat framed by . . . a bright red umbrella! Leafless trees and sculpted statues stood endlessly behind like sentinels of time. She looked for the title of the painting—could it be *Ogmo's Wisdom*? No, the artist had named it *Almost Winter*.

Beside that, another painting—swirling oak leaves, a chaos of faces and figures, and in the center . . . an enormous oak door. A lady with flowing hair rested one hand on the door—in the other she held an hourglass. Her gaze locked on anyone who might approach.

Beside the painting, to the left of the door in the painting, as real as

Leafless trees and sculpted statues stood endlessly behind like sentinels of time.

rainbows, there stood another door. A closet perhaps. The guard had said the museum had no exit doors in the gallery halls. Or had he said no doors period? Perhaps the painting hung there precisely because of the door—artists can be very particular about such things. The door, unadorned, gave no indication of purpose. It did not say "Closed" or "Do Not Open" or "Emergency Exit Only" or anything else like that. It said nothing at all.

Maybe the door is supposed to be open, Laney thought. She could ask, but she imagined a guard would say, "Don't touch anything!" and that would not do. Besides, except for Laney, this gallery hall remained empty—no guard in sight. If the door was not meant to be opened, it would not be a door, or surely it would say so, in some manner, or it would be locked—was it locked? She turned the handle, and the latch bolt retracted.

She opened the door.

www.ingramcontent.com/pod-product-compliance
Lightning Source LLC
Chambersburg PA
CBHW081131300726
48982CB00005B/932

* 9 7 8 1 9 3 6 7 7 2 2 2 3 *